JAY'S GUIDE TO CRUSHING IT

RUBY CLYDE

SCHOLASTIC

Published in the UK by Scholastic, 2023
1 London Bridge, London, SE1 9BG
Scholastic Ireland, 89E Lagan Road, Dublin Industrial Estate,
Glasnevin, Dublin, D11 HP5F

SCHOLASTIC and associated logos are trademarks and/or
registered trademarks of Scholastic Inc.

Text © Ruby Clyde, 2023
Cover illustration by Jess Vosseteig © Scholastic, 2023

The right of Ruby Clyde to be identified
as the author of this work has been asserted by them
under the Copyright, Designs and Patents Act 1988.

ISBN 978 0702 32507 6

A CIP catalogue record for this book
is available from the British Library.

Printed and bound in Great Britain by Clays Ltd, Elcograf S.p.A
Paper made from wood grown in sustainable forests
and other controlled sources.

1 3 5 7 9 10 8 6 4 2

www.scholastic.co.uk

For June, who accepted everybody and cracked me up.

AUTUMN

CHAPTER 1

I look terrible. And I'm not saying that in a dramatic, *I'm-so-ugly* fourteen-year-old way. I'm simply being honest.

"You look lovely," Mum says, smiling.

I look in the mirror again. Cheap black ballet pumps with those tiny string bows on, like tragic little presents. My school skirt is hitting mid-shin and mid-chest, in the range that makes you look like a sack that's decided to further its education. My white button-up shirt is tucked in neatly and it looks like I have no torso. My hair is in that horrible stage of growing out where you look like all four of The Beatles, and no matter what I do it's falling in front of my face like it's trying to hide me. I look terrible.

Jamie walks into the room.

"Oh my god, you look terrible."

"Jamie!" Mum scolds.

"Sorry!"

"He has a point, Mum."

"He does not. You look beautiful."

I can't help thinking that even Mum doesn't really believe this. Being beautiful is a huge hobby of hers. Her dyed blonde hair is always in soft bouncy waves. I've hardly ever seen her without make-up, even when swimming, somehow. Right now, she's wearing a silky gold V neck thing tucked into a black skirt. How is *anyone* this put together at eight in the morning? She looks like a lawyer in a TV series, not a part-time HR manager who works from home. Meanwhile I'm wearing a skirt that belongs in a convent; it doesn't feel like we're working with the same definition of "beautiful". Maybe she just thinks this is a step in the right direction.

"*I'd* look better in it." Jamie sniggers, and Mum chases him out of the room. Honestly, I think he's right. He has longer legs.

"Don't listen to him, Jennifer."

I don't like Mum's new insistence on referring to me by the whole of my name. But she is encouraging a total overhaul of my style and personality, so I guess it makes sense.

"Mum, are we *sure* about the skirt?"

"It's the uniform, and it looks so lovely on you."

"Maybe trousers would be better—"

"It looks lovely," Mum repeats, like things will become lovely if she keeps saying they're lovely, and her mouth has pressed itself into a hard line. That means, "We're not talking about this any more and if you say anything else I'm going to cry and I won't stop for hours and it will be all your fault". So I don't say anything else. "You're going to have the best first day!" she says firmly.

Come on, the first day of school is never *the best*. Imagine how terrible the rest of your life would have to be for the first day of school to even make the top ten. There's nothing worse than standing in a room full of strangers trying to think of a Fun Fact to share about yourself. *Of course* the teacher will ask you for a Fun Fact, and *of course* you won't be able to think of one.

But I've paused for too long, and Mum looks like she might cry.

"The best!" I say, over-enthusiastically. Mum smiles again and it feels like the crisis has been averted.

"Jamie!" she calls. "Get ready to go!"

He slopes back into the room. Jamie actually *does* look good. I don't want to sound jealous, but he looks like I want to look, and I'm literally jealous. He's a tiny bit (a TINY bit) taller than me, and his dark hair is short on the back and sides with the top a little longer and brushed back out of his eyes. We're similar, but sometimes it feels like everything's easy for him: he's confident, goofy, impossible to embarrass (and we're siblings, I've tried – hard), good at getting what he wants, and no one ever seems to think he's doing everything wrong. In fact, most people seem to like him immediately. Most irritatingly he's my favourite person, so I can't even be annoyed at him for it. Still, I glare at his tie and trousers and plain black shoes without ridiculous little bows. Boys get all the luck.

"Have an amazing time," Mum says, kissing us both on the cheek and sending us out the door.

We only moved in a week ago, and Jamie and I have to squeeze past packing boxes to make it out of the house and on to our new street. This is Hatch Heath, our new town. In our neighbourhood the cute little houses are spaced out, surrounded by their own patches of green, with orange and red fallen leaves scattered over everything. Ivy crawls up the houses and flower beds pop with colour along the pavements. It's almost *too* wholesome. This town is so cute it must have cults. Why am I so cynical? Well. I have some theories. But it's so different from London, where we used to live. I can't really get used to having an actual house, and a garden, and none of the buildings being taller than three storeys. You wouldn't think you'd miss high-rises, but then they're gone and suddenly the sky looks too big.

"Sorry I said you look terrible," says Jamie, once we're safely out of Mum's earshot.

"Oh, it's so fine. I really do."

"Seeing you in a skirt is *so* weird."

"It's not my go-to style choice, sure, but maybe I'll get used to it." I'm trying to sound positive, but I absolutely fail. We walk in silence for a while.

"I don't wanna gooooo," Jamie groans.

"Me neither."

"Why would you have a boys' and a girls' school instead of just one large school? Why do they need to split us up? It's not boxing."

"Hey, maybe they *were* all boxing and that's why they split them up."

I'm nervous about being split up, too. We weren't in the same class at our old school, but we hung out during every break and lunch, and always had the same group of friends. Mum didn't really like that, that I was always with boys. I guess literal segregation solves that particular issue. At least it's a short walk to school from our new house. Heath Boys and – you guessed it – Heath Girls are across the street from each other. Kids are crowding in, boys on one side and girls on the other, shouting things across the road and trying to look at each other without seeming like they're looking at each other. I'm starting to panic.

So, I read this self-help book about anxiety once because I'm a super chill and laid-back person, and it suggested trying to be "rational" when you feel anxious about something. I thought it was pretty obvious advice, so, sure, it's worth a go. Because right now all I'm thinking is…

THE TOP FIVE WORST THINGS THAT COULD HAPPEN ON MY FIRST DAY AT SCHOOL

1. Everybody hates me.
2. Everybody thinks I'm weird.
3. When the teacher asks for my Fun Fact, I can't think of one.
4. Everyone finds out what happened at my last school.
5. Everyone thinks I look terrible in this skirt.

So the book would suggest I try to find a "rational response to these worries".

Here goes:

1. Everyone hated me before, what's the difference?
2. Everyone thought I was weird before, what's the difference?
3. You know they're going to ask for a Fun Fact! Just think of one now!
4. Unlikely, I'd barely had social media for five minutes before Mum made me get rid of it. And my phone. Actually, people will definitely think that's weird too.
5. *I* think I look terrible in this skirt. We'll have something in common.

Comforting? Not entirely.

"Well, here we go," says Jamie. "Hang in there."

"Where does that saying come from? A cliff-related incident?"

"Probably. Isn't that a nice bit of perspective?"

He waves and walks into the boys' school, leaving me standing in front of the girls' one. The two schools look identical, with red brick walls dotted with white window frames and surrounded by playing fields – unlike my old school, which looked like a depressing warehouse, even though it was only one of those things. The only difference is the signs in front of each school by the steps leading up to each entrance. Gold letters carved on to red painted wood: Heath Boys and Heath Girls. Well, at least they kept it simple with signs and didn't put a giant pink bow on the girls' school and a moustache on the boys'.

I have to say, Heath Girls looks … kind of nice? It looks like it's been cleaned in the recent past, and I can see kids playing football and basketball in the distance. Who knew brightening a school up would be as simple as actually letting grass grow … and not building it directly in between a supermarket and a pawn shop that was definitely a front for something sketchy.

My form room is easy to find. I can feel people looking at me, but I don't look back at them. Not in the eyes, anyway. I can't stop looking at everybody else's skirts. Not in a creepy way, just in a *how-do-they-look-so-normal-*

in-them-when-I-look-so-weird way. Sometimes it feels like maybe when we were kids they handed out a leaflet about how to wear girls' clothes, and they just never got around to giving one to me. How do I get it so wrong? We all have legs.

I like the teacher, Ms George, on sight. She has a springy walk and her hair jumps energetically in time with her feet. She assigns me a desk at the front. The room fills up, and a pretty girl – who looks extremely normal in a skirt – bounces in and sits next to me. Really pretty, in fact. Her hair is in braids and pulled up into a ponytail situation. She has a tiny hint of orange eyeshadow around her eyes, which stands out against her dark brown skin and matches the orange stones in her pierced ears. She has a bright smile and dimples, and I have a sudden urge to tell her she looks delightful, which I thankfully do not give in to.

"I'm Mina," she tells me. "You must be Jennifer."

"Jay," I tell her out of reflex, realizing too late that Mum would hate it if she found out.

"I'm your Buddy," she says.

"Oh," I say. A bit intense, but OK. "Um, thanks. This is moving fast, but it's nice to have a buddy."

She laughs.

"No, I'm your 'Buddy'; it's, like, a mentoring programme for new students. We're meant to hang out, and I'll take you to your classes."

"Oh, right! Sorry. Did she force you into it?" I ask, nodding at Ms George.

"No, I volunteered," she says, smiling.

I'm suspicious. Why would she do that? "You must be very helpful."

"I'm extremely helpful." Is she teasing me? I think she's teasing me.

"Good morning, everyone!" Ms George cuts across the class' chatter "We have a new student joining us today. This is Jennifer."

"She prefers Jay," Mina chirps.

Great. I've broken one of Mum's new rules ten minutes into the day.

"Jay is joining us from a school in London. Her family are new in town, so let's give her a warm welcome!" Complete silence. "Jay, why don't you tell us a Fun Fact about yourself?"

Did I know it was coming? Yes!

Did I think of a Fun Fact? No!

"Um. OK. I, uh…"

"Stand up so everyone can see you," Ms George says. She says it with an encouraging smile, but right now I want to sue her for emotional damages. Making me stand so everyone can see my nun-skirt is cruelty. I do a sort of half-stand, half-lean on my desk. "Hi, I'm Jay," I start, "and … sorry, what did you want me to say?"

There are some giggles.

"Just a fun fact! Like, what's your favourite book? Or your favourite sport?"

My favourite sport. I know exactly what I would have said a few months ago:

"Great question! I've been skateboarding since I was seven."

"Seven?" that blonde girl at the back of the room gasps. "Wow! You must be really good."

I shrug modestly. "I'm not bad."

"Can you do any tricks?" Mina asks, her eyes shining with awe.

"Oh, you know, kickflips, heelflips, tre flips…"

"Cool!" the class exclaims as one, and we all head down to a skatepark and get pizza and ice cream and—

"Jay?"

Quick, think of something! But I've already broken Mum's first rule since the whole class thinks my name is Jay, so there's no way I can break the second rule: no more skateboarding.

"Running," I say.

"Running?"

"Running."

"What do you like about running?" Ms George asks, desperately trying to coax something out of me.

"It's like walking but faster, what's not to love?"

Great. That's about the weirdest thing I could have said.

Mina bursts out laughing, and the rest of the class joins in. But it's not mean laughing; they seem to think I've intentionally said something funny.

*

12

I know the first day of school is meant to be memorable, but the whole morning ends up being a blur. I feel like my brain is on fast forward. I can't remember anyone's names. Some of the classes are confusing because my old school did a different curriculum. It feels like the place is entirely made out of hallways, and I can't remember how to get anywhere. But Mina stays with me, which makes me feel better. She's funny. And cool. I wonder why she isn't hanging out with her own non-prescription friends.

We can't talk much through our lessons, but we sit together at lunch. That's when the questions start.

"So, tell me all about your old school."

"Oh – you know, it was kind of like this one."

"Do you miss it?"

"Not really." Time to change the subject. "Tell me about this place. What can I expect from my time as a student of Heath Girls?"

Mina grins and puts on her best tour guide voice: "Well! If you look to your left, you'll see some of your fellow Heathians enjoying the most popular local pastime, trying to catch a glimpse of the students over at Heath Boys." She waves towards a group of girls by the gates, peeking across the road and giggling.

"Wow! I wonder if *I'll* ever see one."

"Maybe, if you're lucky! Over there, at the table by the windows, you'll see the queens of our year, led by Dani Hex."

I can tell who she means immediately: the fourteen-year-old who looks like she has a personal stylist. I wonder why Mina isn't sitting with them; she also gives me popular girl energy.

"Hex. Like H-E-X? Like a curse?"

"Mm. Apparently it's Belgian, and not just a warning."

Dani shoots a dirty look at Mina when she catches us looking. There's obviously some history there, and I wish I knew Mina well enough to ask what it is.

"I'll be sure never to cross her royal highness."

"And finally, you might have spotted the photos all over the school."

I haven't – I've generally been too busy trying not to do something humiliating that everyone will remember for ever – but now that she mentions it, I notice there are photos all over the dining room of girls in nice dresses and boys in suits. The one closest to me has a placard under it that says *Summer Dance 2018: Under The Sea*. Everyone's wearing blue or green and some people have little ocean accessories, like clamshell bags. One girl is wearing a sort of lobster hat, which against the odds really suits her.

"You're looking at the highlight of the Heath school year: the Summer Dance. Every year has a different theme, but it's basically an excuse for Heath girls and boys to get all dressed up and try to kiss each other."

"That sounds terrifying." Mina thinks I'm joking, but I am not.

"Don't worry. You've got the whole school year left to pick out a dress."

Great! Something new to dread!

When the bell for the end of the day rings, we all spill out on to the street outside. Me and Mina are hanging out by the gate to wait for my brother when I hear it: the rasp of wheels on concrete and the snap of wood hitting the ground. I spin around in time to see someone come careening out of the boys' school on a skateboard.

He's got that kind of aggressive style some skaters have – like he's about to crash into something at any moment. He swerves into the road, sloppy and reckless, but super fast and bold. His shiny black hair is floppy and his tie is loose around his neck; he hasn't bothered with a blazer. He has headphones on and his school shirt is stained with ink.

He is, hands down, the coolest boy I've ever seen.

And I miss skateboarding *so much*.

"I see you've spotted Alex, the whole world's crush," Mina says with a teasingly raised eyebrow.

I feel my face get hot. I definitely look like a girl with a crush, not just a casual fan of extreme sports.

"I'm just worried; he looks like he's going to get run over." Really I'm watching him ollie up a kerb. He gets more height than I do, but I think I'm more precise…

"That actually happened last year. The car wasn't going fast, but I hope it was a learning experience."

"Is he *your* crush, then?"

"He's not my type," Mina says, laughing.

"Just the rest of the world's?"

"Exactly."

I try to tear my eyes away from Alex, who is now getting yelled at by someone he's nearly crashed into. He doesn't even notice, just keeps riding. *Stop watching him. No more skating; Mum would have a breakdown.*

Jamie comes over to join us, leaving a group of boys laughing at whatever joke he's just told. *How* does he already have a whole posse? Probably because he doesn't call them his posse.

"Jay! Did you see the skater? He's *good*."

"Right?!" I say. "He kind of reminds me of a young Nyjah Huston, just loads of speed and height and no fear of physical consequences—"

"Oh, you're into skateboarding?" Mina asks, snapping me out of our analysis in time to remember once again that I am *not supposed to be into skateboarding any more.*

"She is, she's really good!" Jamie says, then suddenly remembers too. "I mean, no, she's not. What?"

Mina blinks. "What?"

"This is my brother, Jamie," I say quickly. "He's joking. Jamie, this is Mina."

"Hi, Mina," he says, looking embarrassed.

"Let's go, Jamie!" I say. "See you tomorrow, Mina!"

"Nice to meet you!" Jamie calls back as we walk quickly

away. He glances at me. "Sorry. I keep forgetting the details of this whole 'fresh start' thing…"

"Me too. My whole class already calls me Jay."

Jamie grimaces. "Strike one."

"Yup. So, uh, if there's a skater … I guess there's probably a skatepark in town."

"I met him today, he's in my year. His name's Alex. Apparently there's a skatepark on the other side of that big park by the house."

"Oh, cool," I say. There's a pause while I try to stop imagining what the skatepark might be like.

Jamie looks over at me, looking uncharacteristically nervous. "There's something I need to tell you."

"You mean there's somehow information about you that I still don't know? I have doubts."

"It's not about me." He takes a deep breath, then says, "I saved your skateboard."

I stop walking and stare at him. "What?"

"When … everything got thrown out…"

My fists clench at the memory. Standing in front of our old block of flats while Mum loaded my skateboard into her car, next to bags of my clothes, shoes and posters. It was just before we moved, and it was the last hot day of the summer; I wanted to tear off the cast that was still on my arm. I wanted to cry, too, but I couldn't. Instead, I just nodded when Mum said it was good to have a fresh start, and that I'd really grown out of all that stuff anyway.

Thinking about that day always makes me want to throw up. But whatever, that's the past now! The past can't make you throw up unless you're eating food from it.

"I knew she'd take it all to the charity shop on the high street, so I went straight down there and bought it back. I hid it in my mattress and she moved it to Hatch Heath with us without even knowing."

Jamie has me utterly lost for words. The boy has always had a touch of the criminal mastermind to him, and he's always been less scared of upsetting Mum than I am. He's the inventor of Homework Club, the imaginary but very respectable after-school studying collective we pretend to attend when we want to do something without her knowing. He's a master at forging a sick note, benevolently handing them out to anyone who doesn't want to do PE. He's the reason we've seen so many horror films, by buying tickets for kids' movies and sneaking into the other screen part way through. Sure, we both had more fun the time we just stayed and watched *Encanto*, but the point is he excels at trickery.

"It's just … I knew you didn't really want to give it up," Jamie says quietly.

He's right. I didn't. Handing over my skateboard had felt like handing over a piece of myself. But especially on that day I had been kind of thinking: maybe Mum's right. I don't look like anyone else I know. And I got hurt, badly, because of that and my skateboard. And when I said *hey, maybe I'll try things your way*, she was really happy. And it felt good to see her happy. The thing with Mum is that she doesn't get angry. It's worse. Jamie and I call it Sad Mum. She panics. She *cries*. And no matter how much you try you can't comfort her, because you're the reason she's upset. She's always been like that, but after I got hurt – I'd never seen her so devastated. She was so worried about me and she was scared I might get hurt again and, I don't know, it felt kind of good to be able to calm her down for once when it was all my fault. But I miss that skateboard so much…

Jamie is still describing his heist in smug detail. "I unzipped the mattress cover, took the board apart and put the whole thing in there. I even packed some jumpers in around it so it would lay flat. Now it's reassembled, ready to ride, and hidden at the back of my closet. C'mon, be impressed."

"I … I'm *extremely* impressed. You're a genius."

"It's been said."

"But I can't ever use it. You know that. Mum would flip out."

"Jay…" Jamie is looking at me with my least favourite expression: pity. "At some point we should talk about what happened. I know Mum blamed everything on skating, and the way you look, but that's not…"

I hold up a hand because I don't want to hear it, but he keeps going.

"You love skating, you're good at it, you shouldn't give it up—"

"Nope," I say, cutting him off. "Thanks, Jamie, but no." He looks hurt, but I made Mum a promise. "Thanks for saving my skateboard. But you shouldn't have. I don't want it any more."

At least it's a short walk home, so we don't have to spend too long in painful silence.

CHAPTER 2

Me and Jamie just pretend the Rescued Skateboard conversation never happened, so everything goes back to normal there. I start getting used to the new house and to my new relationship with Mum. In the mornings, she tells me I look nice. After school, she asks what the girls in my class are like and laughs at stories about kids spritzing each other with hairspray in the bathrooms. She tells me similar stories about the girls she went to school with. I don't think we've ever had something in common before – it's nice.

And school is weirdly ... good! People are nice to me, and they seem to think I'm funny. Heath Girls is so much smaller than my last school, so it never feels like you could get lost in the crowd. I thought that would feel too exposing, but it feels like being part of a group. Maybe fitting in Mum's way *is* good.

Mostly, school is good because of Mina. I suspect we might be becoming … friends?

I know it sounds unlikely, but hear me out: first of all, we like all the same classes. Well, she likes *all* our classes, so of course there's some crossover: history. What I'm saying is we both like history. We sit next to each other in every class except for biology, and then she asks to swap so we can sit next to each other anyway. All we've talked about so far is school, but we laugh a lot while we do it. It definitely has all the markers of friendship, though part of me still can't quite believe it.

I know I'm being paranoid, I'm just not used to having friends like Mina. Basically, she looks like the kind of girl my mum wants me to look like, and I've always assumed that girls like that would probably hang out with other girls like that. Like how magpies hang out with other magpies, but kind of give pigeons the cold shoulder. Do birds have shoulders? OK, I get that it's not rational to believe someone doesn't want to be your friend when they're acting like they do. That anxiety book I mentioned earlier would tell me to break down my thought process so I can see how illogical it really is. Well, here goes:

WHY I DON'T THINK MINA WANTS TO BE MY FRIEND EVEN THOUGH SHE IS ACTIVELY BEING MY FRIEND

1. She's cool, so she could have other, cooler friends instead of me if she wanted.
2. She probably just feels like she has to be nice to me because I seem like a loser.
3. People probably think I'm weird.
4. That means they'll think she's weird by association.
5. She probably doesn't want people to think she's weird.

Actually, that all looks pretty logical to me.

Mum is thrilled when I tell her about Mina.

"That's fantastic! Why don't you bring her over for dinner? Just tell me which day. And what kind of food she likes."

She smiles at me, and I smile back. It's cool that she wants to meet Mina. Mum looks very friendly and happy today. She's wearing a red jumper that's kind of a dress at the same time (?), which makes her look like a tall strawberry. I think that might not technically be a compliment, though, so instead I say, "Nice dress!"

She beams. I've always kind of wished we could get to know each other, and that she'd like my friends and hobbies. Maybe I just never gave her the chance.

"Thank goodness you've outgrown that horrible group of boys."

Oh.

"Freddie, Jack and Omar?" Jamie says, leaning into the kitchen. "They're not horrible!"

They're not. And I haven't exactly outgrown them, I've just been moved to an entirely different location and had my phone taken away. I've outgrown them in the way you'd outgrow your family if you got kidnapped.

"You're right, darling," she says. "I didn't mean that. But it's important for girls to have female friends, who they can have proper conversations with."

Maybe she has a point. Freddie, Jack, Omar and I didn't have proper conversations. We just skated, and sometimes we'd go to someone's house and drink energy drinks and play video games. I couldn't tell you anything about their hopes, dreams or feelings. It was nice.

"I'm still in touch with all my girls from school," Mum continues, "so you never know, Mina could still be around when you're my age!"

I try to imagine me and Mina going for massages and yoga classes together in twenty years like Mum and her friends back in London did, which really seems like quite a big commitment at this stage. I think she's just so excited I'm friends with a girl that she wants to handcuff her to me so she can't leave.

"Well, let's slow down; we haven't hung out off school premises yet."

Mum laughs, but she looks pleased. "Seriously, sweetheart," she says, "it's not easy making new friends. You're doing really well, and you've grown up so much since we moved. I'm proud of you."

I mean, I'm still fourteen, just as I was when we moved here, but how nice is that? She's proud of me.

By Friday, I'm feeling like the perfect daughter. I've made it through my first week at a new school without any *incidents*. I've made friends (I think) with a girl. I've worn The Skirt every single day – Mina has even shown me how to roll it up a bit to make it look more normal. I mean, it still doesn't look normal on me *at all*, but at least it objectively looks more like the skirts the other girls wear. I'm even feeling better about my hair. The trick has been to not look at it when I'm near a reflective surface. Mum hasn't cried once. It's been a good week.

And then on Friday, just before lunch, I'm in PE. Which is never a good start to a story. I'm pretty athletic, and I *still* find PE absolutely horrifying. Who wants to put on tiny shorts and be forced to do drills by someone who's so average at sports they had to come play netball with teenagers?

This PE teacher's first name is Hugo. I know that because he said, "Call me Hugo," rather than Mr Smith or Coach Smith or whatever. He's younger than most teachers, and some of the girls say how cute he is. I don't like him, though, because it feels like he wants us to think he's cool (see: asking us to call him Hugo), which I personally think is a sign of weakness in a teacher. Then, as I'm minding my own business and doing some push-ups, he suddenly squats down beside me.

"Don't worry if this is too hard on your arm, Jennifer!"

I feel a spike of adrenaline. How does he even know my arm has been broken? And did anybody else hear him say that?

I spend the rest of the class on edge. When I'm finally changed and trying to follow Mina to lunch, he calls me back.

"Jennifer! Stay behind for a quick chat?"

Mina gives me a confused look.

"I'll save you a seat, Jay."

Hugo closes the door behind her and we're alone in the gym. "How about a glass of squash?"

"OK," I say, feeling like the squash is somehow a trap.

"So, Jennifer," he says, once we're awkwardly sitting at opposite ends of a low bench and I have a small plastic cup of orange squash, "as you know, I'm your Head of Year."

"As I know." I nod. I did not know. I haven't really been keeping abreast of everyone's job titles.

"I'm like a captain or a team leader, and I'm always here to help. I thought it might be nice if we set aside some time for a little chat each week after PE. Sound good?" He doesn't pause for me to answer. "How are you getting on?

You had a bit of a time of it at your last school, didn't you?" He reaches into a backpack and takes out a folder, which I suspect contains my full academic and personal history. It feels like a threat, like he's going to open it and fact-check me about my own life.

"It wasn't that bad."

The folder swings open.

"A broken arm and a concussion sounds pretty bad to me."

"I don't want to talk about it."

"I understand," he says. He does not. "But that's exactly why you should! I chatted to your mum on the phone to check in yesterday, and she says you've been making a really great fresh start here. I just want to make sure that continues!"

So she's been telling him about me. I guess it makes sense that she'd talk to my Head of Year, but it makes me feel weird. I look at him in silence.

"Lots of people experience bullying," he says.

If anything I'm getting *more* silent.

"I noticed your friend called you Jay," he goes on. "Your mum said you were trying to leave that old nickname behind?"

I'm still deeply silent, but Hugo is talking away for the both of us.

"You know, it's *really* common for girls to have a tomboy phase!" he says perkily. "And it's *really* common to leave that behind once you become a teenager. You shouldn't feel like you have to keep using that nickname just because it's what you're used to! This is a great chance for you to reinvent yourself."

I shrug. What I want to say is why is *everyone* so excited that I said I'd try growing out my short back and sides? Mum's running around spreading the good news to Hugo. Hugo also seems thrilled and he doesn't know a single other thing about me, other than that I'm moving on from my "tomboy phase". Calling it that doesn't feel right. But maybe that's the thing about being a teenager: you don't realize your phases are phases? Mum's gone into overdrive since what happened at my last school, but she'd wanted me to move on from my "phase" for a long time. I guess she was always thinking about how to keep me safe, and then her worst fears came true. It's nice that she wants me to have someone to talk to. Right? And then I remember I haven't said any of this out loud and I am not talking to the someone she has sent. I can feel Hugo getting impatient. Lunch is nearly over.

"Can I go?" I ask.

He sighs. "Sure."

I head straight to Sociology and slide into my seat next to Mina.

"Where were you?" she asks. "I was lonely. I had to sit in the library and pretend that I know how to read."

"Drama queen. We both know you learned months ago.

Apparently I have to do catch-up sessions for stuff I might have missed when I switched."

She looks at me. "With a PE teacher?"

"He's actually our Head of Year, Mina. Please address him by his proper title."

Mina snorts. "Isn't his proper title 'Call-Me-Hugo'?"

I giggle, and for the rest of the lesson Mina occasionally slips into an impression of Hugo to make me laugh.

Friday afternoon has everyone buzzing around outside the gates, spilling into the road while the girls and boys mingle. I'm waiting for Jamie and chatting to Mina, but really I'm looking for Alex, the cool skater boy. It's become a habit, really. I watch as he comes speeding into the road again, backpack swinging wildly as he tries to put his arms through the straps while still skating as fast as he can. I watch the look of total concentration on his face, like the only thing in the world is his skateboard.

I know that feeling. Suddenly I miss it so badly I feel homesick.

Mum thinks I want to leave who I was behind. I want Mum to be happy – but I want that feeling back. And then I have a genius thought. *What she doesn't know can't hurt her.* Maybe I can have it both ways. Maybe I can be who my mum wants me to be in public without giving everything up. I'm already hiding so many things about myself – what's one more thing?

I see Jamie saying goodbye to his new friends and tell Mina I'll see her on Monday. As we start walking home, he takes one look at my face and says, "OK, what's going on?"

"Still got my skateboard?"

He grins. "Of course."

"Great. I'm going to need it."

Jamie whoops and jumps into the air.

We use the weekend to plan.

"OK," Jamie says, pacing his room, in his element, while I sit at his desk. "The simplest solution is often the best. The skatepark is only ten minutes away. If you set your alarm, you can be down there by five a.m., and get back before school. I'd suggest weekdays only, because we can guarantee she'll be in the house waiting to send us off to school. But of course, *someone* could still see you. I don't think anyone from school will be out there that early, but Mum's already joined a yoga class. I assume yoga ladies like to be up with the sun. It just takes one of them seeing you skating and saying, 'I didn't know your daughter was so sporty!'" Jamie shudders. "The fallout would be ... devastating."

"You're right, though I think we're speculating heavily about what yoga ladies do," I say, taking the floor. "But what if they didn't see *me*?"

He stares. "Are you planning to put a fence up around the skatepark or something? I don't think that would work.

Well, actually, how big is the skatepark? I wonder how much fencing you'd need..."

"Think smarter, not harder, Jamie," I say. I pick up one of his caps from the edge of his desk. I put it on, pushing my hair off my face and tucking it under the hat so you can't tell that it's long.

He smiles. "You look like yourself again."

"Now imagine this with jeans and a hoodie. *We* know I look like myself – but to a stranger..."

"... you look like a boy!" He applauds, and I give a little bow.

"We just have to hope that no one who knows me sees me up close. And what are the odds of anyone else being in the skatepark at five a.m.?"

"Oh, it's bold. I love it."

"What do I say if someone starts talking to me, though?"

"Oh, just lie."

"Lie?"

"Yeah, it's like the opposite of the truth."

I roll my eyes.

"The trick to a good lie, Jay," Jamie says in his best teacher voice, "is to include a little bit of the truth. You just moved here from London. You're homeschooled. You only skate early in the mornings because your mum doesn't approve of it since you broke your arm. Hmm. Maybe your mum is really religious, or something – that adds to the homeschool angle..."

I hold up my hand to stop him before he gets carried away by his story. I'm not as cool under pressure as he is, so I probably won't be going with a lie quite as elaborate as "homeschooled religious skateboarder", but it's so unlikely I'll have to say anything anyway. No one's going to find out. And I just want to skate again.

"I've decided: Monday will be day one of the double life."

"I have never respected you more. This is daring and elaborate, and I'm proud."

"Thanks. And … thank you for saving my board. I'm sorry I was weird about it at first."

"It's OK." He hesitates, then says, "You know that none of the stuff that happened was because of skateboarding, right?"

I nod. It wasn't because of skateboarding. But it was because of me. So I'll just keep this side of me hidden. *Easy.* Why doesn't everybody repress stuff all the time?

CHAPTER 3

The rest of the weekend is nice. On Saturday we have my favourite food for dinner. (Pepperoni pizza. I know that's not that exciting, but why mess with perfection?) On Sunday Mum lets me choose which movie we watch. She's acting like I've won an award or something.

The mayor places the medal around my neck and the crowd gathered in the town square cheer. He smiles at me proudly.

"Congratulations, Jay. You did it. You saved the town."

"Actually, I just agreed to wear a skirt and stop skateboarding."

"Oh. Seriously? That's actually not going to have that much of an impact on the town."

He takes the medal back.

In a way, it *isn't* a big deal. I've just changed my clothes and hair a bit. And maybe Mum's right that looking like this is safer because nothing like what happened at my last school has happened so far. So why is it so hard to keep up? Why am I so tired? Why am I so excited to be myself again? Finally, Monday rolls around. If someone had told me to wake up at 5 a.m. for any other reason, I would have objected. I'd have snoozed the alarm several times before stumbling out of bed and seeking out some coffee, which I don't even drink because I'm fourteen. But on Monday morning when the phone I've borrowed from Jamie starts vibrating under my pillow, I spring up (silently, of course). From the streetlights outside I can just see enough to get ready.

Then, and I think this might be the part I'm most excited about, I slide my skateboard out from under my bed, the wheels whispering on the carpet.

I run my hands over the rough, sandpapery grip tape on top of the board. Mine is black (you can get it in other colours, but to be honest, I think anything other than black is tacky). You can see scuff marks where my feet have made the same motions over and over. On the underside of the board is smooth wood with a design, though mine's all scratched up now from grinding along rails and scraping on concrete. It's a pink logo from a skate company called Girl. Jamie got it for me for Christmas last year. We both thought it was hilarious because people were always asking

34

if I was a boy or a girl at the skatepark, so I could flip the board upside down and say, "Well, the *board's* a girl." OK, it made *us* laugh, and my brother and I are my most important audience.

There are so many parts that make up a skateboard – wheels, bearings, trucks, bushings – and every single one of those things can change how riding the board feels. It took me a long time to get all the specifics right, but now my board is exactly how I want it. I can't believe I almost let it go; I was just so angry and embarrassed about the … incident. Mum didn't understand what a big deal it was when I said I'd get rid of it. She thinks skateboards are just toys and that all of them are exactly the same – but mine is like a part of me.

On top of the skateboard is a stack of clothes Jamie has given me: jeans which are a little small for him and fit fine if I roll them up, a T-shirt, a pullover hoodie and a beanie to hide my hair under. On my feet I wear the white trainers Mum bought me for PE. I'll just have to keep them hidden from her once skateboarding inevitably wears them down and rips holes in them.

In the faint light, wearing my new clothes, I study myself in the mirror. I actually like what I see. I look *good*. Seriously. Even though I'm technically in disguise, I don't look like I'm wearing a costume.

You really would think I was a boy if you saw me. I'm still totally flat chested, which I don't really know how to feel about. At my old school people were starting to tease girls who didn't have boobs yet, so sometimes I wished they would just grow. But sometimes I have dreams where I wake up and my chest is, like, comedy big. Like I'm smuggling basketballs under my T-shirt. I hate it. Luckily that hasn't happened yet. Things to be grateful for, right?

I open the window I greased with olive oil the night before (maybe a bad idea, my room smells like salad). I climb out to the patch of grass outside our house, skateboard in one hand, careful not to knock it against anything. At any moment, this could go so wrong. Our new house has two floors, with the living room, kitchen, bathroom and mine and Jamie's rooms on the ground floor. Another bathroom, Mum's home office and bedroom are on the second – directly above mine. Her curtains are drawn, no light on.

If Mum sees me now, she'll probably never let me out of the house again. But I manage to ease the window back down and take off down the street without a single sound. It's ten past five. Ten minutes to the skatepark, ten minutes back. I have to be home before our alarms go off at seven. That gives me over an hour at the skatepark.

When I'm far enough away from the houses on our street I run on to my board. The feeling is *incredible*. It's been almost four months and I was worried I'd have lost my skills, but everything comes straight back to me as I carve across the asphalt and ollie up a kerb. An ollie, technically, is when you do a jump with your skateboard.

You snap the tail of your board against the ground and roll your front foot upwards to jerk yourself into the air. It's, like, Skateboarding 101, but when you get really good at them you *fly*. I'd seriously suggest that if you don't know how to do one, you learn so you get a chance to feel that feeling.

Soon I'm barrelling into the park, heading towards the far end where the skatepark is. Honestly, I'd be happy with just a piece of wood leaning on a brick, but fortunately it's way better than that. There's a quarter pipe, a bank, a ledge, a mini ramp and a funbox with a rail. I know "funbox" sounds like it's going to be a box full of surprising treats, but it's actually just three ramps leading up to a square platform in the middle with a rail sloping down one side. Once you know how to skate a funbox it really is … well, fun.

At first I just carve up and down all the ramps, getting to know the place and enjoying the feel of a board under my feet. Skating in the park, wearing my brother's clothes, I feel like … myself. Not like the awkward skirt-clad Heath Girls' student I'm pretending to be for Mum.

I don't want to think about Mum just now.

I decide to start this session off with my favourite trick ever … *the tre flip*.

WHY I LOVE TRE FLIPS

1. It's a kickflip (where your board rolls over in the air underneath you) combined with a three-sixty pop shove it (where your board spins all the way around in the air underneath you). Good trick + good trick = REALLY COOL TRICK.
2. Not to show off, but they aren't that easy. Not everybody can do them.
3. Actually, 1 & 2 sum it all up.

It takes me a couple of goes, but eventually I stick the landing on a tre flip over the funbox.

And then I hear something.

The unmistakable sound of a board's front wheels slapping the concrete.

It's a familiar sound. It's how skaters congratulate each other, like a tiny, laid-back round of applause. It's nice hearing it now, because, you know, we all enjoy recognition – but it's also a little unnerving, because it means I'm not alone in the skatepark where I've assumed a false identity. I feel like I know who it's going to be before I even turn around.

I turn slowly, like that thing that happens in movies where a character says "he's behind me, isn't he?" and turns around and he totally is.

Yep. Alex. What did Mina call him? "The whole world's crush." He definitely looks the part. His school shirt, tie and backpack are lying on the ground next to him, with a beaten-up copy of a book called *On the Road*. I haven't heard of it, but I can see the word "Classic" on the cover so I assume it's smart. He's wearing a Patagonia T-shirt that's so faded I can barely read the logo. The floppy hair is flopping.

"That was sick," he says.

I stand in frozen anxious silence before I realize I'm going to have to at least say something.

"Thanks, man," I say.

"Cool, man," he says, before bombing down a ramp and ollying over the funbox so aggressively I'm sure his board will snap.

My first instinct is to sprint from the skatepark and never look back. But Alex doesn't look at me again, just keeps skating. Most importantly he doesn't rip the cap off my head, point at me and scream "She's a woman!" like that one bit in *Mulan*. In fact, I don't think it even crosses his mind that I could be. When a guy in a skatepark thinks you might be a girl – especially a girl who just did a tre flip – he looks at you. He notices. It's just the way it is. It's like if I saw a cat do a tre flip: *I've never seen that before, is that even possible, how dare that cat be better than me?* But when a guy in a skatepark thinks you're a boy, he doesn't think twice about you.

You're just there, in the way that the ramps are there or the clouds are in the sky.

I bet he thinks I'm a boy, and I remember this feeling. I *miss* this feeling. In the skatepark back home I'd have it for a few minutes before one of my friends showed up and said "she" instead of "he" and the stranger I'd been skating with would get awkward and apologize or laugh and say I was "really good for a girl". Here, there's no one to correct the assumption.

Alex and I continue existing in the same place in pleasant silence. I like watching him skate. He's so fast, and he loves doing big air tricks, blasting off the quarter pipe for grabs. It's like he doesn't feel fear. He gets angry, though, kicking his board across the ground when he messes something up. It's kinda funny that skaters do this, because of course it wasn't the board's fault. But the board isn't going to stand up and punch you in the face, so you allow yourself to lash out at it.

We have such different styles, but what's very satisfying is … I think I might be better than him. Look, you can't help but compare yourself to the other skaters when you're in a park. And it's a nice feeling when you measure up.

"So did you just move here?"

Oh god. What did Jamie say? *Lie.* My voice is already on the lower end – should I try to make it deeper? What age do boys' voices break? Maybe he'll just think I'm a late bloomer. "Yeah, from the city. Of London." My voice cracks slightly out of nerves, which might actually be the most convincingly teenage boy thing I could have done.

"Cool. Bet there's better street spots there."

"Yeah, there's some cool spots. Any cool spots here?"

"There's a couple."

We skate in silence some more. Hopefully we're done making small talk; so long as I don't have to attempt the elaborate backstory Jamie suggested, I'll be fine.

"Haven't seen you at school," he says.

"Nah, I'm homeschooled." *Come on.* Now I'm in for it.

"Oh, wow," he says. "Why?"

"Because of religion," I say, realizing in this moment that I haven't actually decided which religion my imaginary devout mother follows. Luckily, it doesn't seem like Alex knows much about religion either.

"That's cool. I didn't know religious people could, like, skateboard and stuff."

"My mum's the religious one, not me."

He nods, like this all makes a lot of sense. "Is that why you're here so early? She doesn't like you skating?"

Jamie's right – letting some of the truth in makes the lies come easier. "Yeah, exactly. What about you?"

"I come here as much as I can. I don't like being at home," he says, looking away. "Skating's all I really care about." He pushes his hair back, showing muscular arms, and rolls away from me again.

I almost start laughing. Not in a mean way, but he's

practically a cliché: the hints of a troubled backstory, the dedication to his sport, the hair. He keeps staring into the distance with a furrowed brow and a look that's very "teen prince who fears the responsibility of ruling the kingdom". Do you know what I mean? I can see why he's thought of as such crush material. Not that that's why I like looking at him, I just like watching him skate. At least, I'm pretty sure that's all it is.

I know what people would think about me: *she likes skateboarding, she dresses like a boy, she doesn't have a crush on her new town's most eligible bachelor: she's totally gay.* That's what everybody at my last school thought, and I always said that I wasn't.

I'm actually kind of embarrassed by the truth, which is … *I don't know.* You're meant to know, aren't you? Especially once you're fourteen. But I've never had a crush on anybody. At least, I don't think I have. When I'm around a boy I feel like we're both just getting on with our own things. When I'm around a girl, I feel like some sort of circus clown. Is *that* a crush? I don't know.

I glance at the watch I've borrowed from Jamie and jump – I have just under ten minutes to get home.

"Later," I say to Alex.

"Later," he says.

I skate back to our street as fast as I can, getting off the board to sprint the last section so nobody hears the wheels. I slip through the window, heart beating fast, and change back into my pyjamas, hiding my skate clothes and board under the bed. I lie down, staring at the ceiling, before all of the alarm clocks in the house go off at once.

Time for school.

As Jamie and I pass each other in the hallway I give him a thumbs up, and he gives me the quietest cheer he can.

Breakfast is tense. At first, I'm paranoid that Mum somehow knows my secret, but I don't think it's that. She keeps asking if I have any plans for Friday. (*School, for the next four years.*) It's not until she asks if any of the teachers have had a "little chat" that I get it.

She wants to find out if I'm speaking to Hugo.

"Yeah, I had a little … chat with my PE teacher – uh, Head of Year – last Friday. His name is Hugo," I say, resigned to the conversation.

"Yes, Hugo – isn't he wonderful?" she says. "I had a few phone calls with him before you started, to ask if he could make sure you settled in all right. After everything that happened, I knew it would be important for you to have a teacher around that you can talk to. He's lovely."

"Yeah," I say, "really nice."

"So you'll keep meeting him?" she asks, fixing me with big, concerned eyes.

"Maybe," I say hesitantly, "if I'm not too busy with … homework and that sort of thing…"

"Jennifer, I think you need to talk to someone about what happened, and about all the changes you're going through.

I just need to know you're OK." Her manicured hands shake slightly around her cup of green tea. I feel like I can see the shimmer of tears in her eyes already. Oh god. Don't cry.

"Sure," I say quickly. She beams and it's like the clouds suddenly go away. I exhale.

"I think it'll be good for you to have a positive male role model around," she says.

Wow. I have to stop myself from laughing out loud. Mum has this theory that it's important for me and Jamie to have "male role models" because her and Dad broke up before I was born and we're not close with him. I've never understood the logic. Does she think I want to look like a boy because I don't know enough boys? Surely bringing more men into my life will just give me more inspiration?

I take a deep breath and push down the anger that's started flaring up whenever I say I'll do something just so Mum doesn't get upset. And then choke back the guilt that comes from getting so angry when I know it's just like she says — she just wants me to be OK; she just wants me to be safe. But still. *I went skating this morning, and Mum has no idea.* She doesn't get to control everything.

Of course, after showering I have to go and put on that horrible skirt and brush my terrible hair. Guess *I* don't get to control everything, either.

*

As soon as we're away from the house, Jamie begins to bounce around me.

"So tell me everything. Is the park big? Did you land anything good? Did anybody see you?"

"It's not huge, but it's nice! Didn't land anything too exciting, but there's a rail I really want to start practising on…"

"Yeah you should definitely get some more rail tricks down, so you can build up to hitting stair rails."

Jamie is the reason I got into skating. When I was seven, really little, him and his friends had a skateboarding phase and he started bringing me along to the skatepark with them. He was an all right skater – but he's pretty good at everything, to be honest, so I guess he gets bored of stuff fast. He'd let me have a go on his board and I was *hooked*. I wasn't good straight away, but I was absolutely determined to get better. In the end Jamie preferred to watch me skate than to skate himself, so he gave me his board and started acting like my manager or something, helping me learn new tricks and encouraging me to try things even if they scared me, or if other guys at the park teased me.

"Oh my god, definitely. Rails are so scary, though. But listen. You asked if I saw anybody…"

He stops.

"Jay. What happened?"

"Well, I did."

"See someone?"

"Yeah."

"For god's sake, who? Who saw you?"

"Skater Alex from your school."

"I guess it does make sense Skater Alex would be at the skatepark. But why at five a.m. if he wasn't even wearing a disguise? Well, actually, I wasn't there – *was* he wearing a disguise?"

"No, though he was wearing a T-shirt that I quite liked. Be honest with me, Jamie: am I doomed?"

"Did he recognize you?"

"No."

"Did he realize you're a girl?"

"No. Well, I'm not sure. He said 'man' a few times, but that might just have been a slang thing, you know?"

"And did you stick to the story?"

"Yes. I told him I was homeschooled and religious, just like you said. Which reminds me actually, at some point we should decide what religion I am."

Jamie nods. "It's a very good lie. Some of my best work." He thinks it over. "This definitely raises the risk level, but so long as he never meets Heath-Girls-Jennifer I think we're safe. Maybe I like this added drama. An extra thrill."

"Risking full Sad Mum and never being allowed to leave the house again isn't thrilling enough for you?"

He lays a comforting hand on my shoulder.

"Don't worry, *I'm* not risking anything. You're the one who would get grounded."

"You provided the skateboard! That's means and motive right there!"

"I'll deny everything and you can prove nothing."

"I promise I will find a way to take you down with me."

Jamie grins. "It's a deal. If you go down, we both go down."

He sticks out his hand. We shake firmly.

In our first class, I sit down in the seat Mina has saved for me. She's wearing these nice little earrings that are like hoops but small. Small hoops. They're silver and I like how they glint under the fluorescent classroom lights. Her eyes kind of glint in the same way when she's about to laugh. Don't worry, I don't say that out loud. Why did I think that? Is THAT a crush? Or is that a normal friend thought?

"So," she says, "what did you get up to this weekend? Excitements? Betrayals? Hot dates?"

"Well," I say, "the usual. Dressed up as a man to practise my favourite extreme sport. Helped Mum with the shopping. Nothing big. You?"

"Yeah, basically the same. Dressed up as a boy to get a job at a law firm, won a couple of embezzlement cases, nothing major."

Of course that didn't happen. I don't even know what embezzlement means.

"We had pizza on Saturday. That was pretty much the highlight. You?"

"Ugh, I didn't even have pizza. My weekend was so *boring*."

Something is really starting to seem strange about Mina. How can someone be this pretty, well-dressed and nice without having anything to do on the weekend?

"What?" she says.

"What?" I realize I've been staring at her with suspicion.

"You look really suspicious."

"I guess I just … thought you would have plans."

"Plans like schemes? Plots? Do you think I'm up to something nefarious?"

"No! Are you?"

"I *obviously* wouldn't tell you."

"That's a very suspicious thing to say, but no, I don't think you're nefarious."

"So what do you mean, you thought I'd have plans?"

She's having way too much fun watching me squirm.

"OK, so I GUESS what I'm saying is that, objectively, you look a little bit like that popular girl you pointed out on my first day. Dani Hex."

"She's white and blonde, Jay; I don't think we look very similar at all."

"Not like that. As in, aesthetically. You wear the same nice trainers. You both have piercings. You wear lip gloss. You're cool, pretty people. The kind of people who have plans. Like hangouts. Parties. Galas? I don't know. Do you know what I'm saying?"

Oh god. Am I trying to compliment her? Is this a compliment? Is that what I'm doing? Why can't I stop? Mina smiles and looks at me sideways.

"Thanks for calling me pretty."

The fluorescent strip lights above us feel like a grill now.

Just then Ms George bustles in, saving me from the most uncomfortable moment I've had in – I don't know – a couple of hours.

"Well, believe it or not, Dani and I actually used to be friends. Really good friends," Mina whispers as she takes out her books.

I *knew* they looked like they matched, somehow!

"But now we're not. I'll tell you more of the saga later," Mina promises.

"There's a saga?!"

"Oh, there's a saga all right."

"I genuinely cannot wait," I whisper back as the class starts.

For the rest of the day, it's like everything in the world is conspiring to stop Mina from telling me the Dani Hex Saga. No, there must be a better name for it. The Tale of Hex? Hex's Tale? Dani's Hex! Every single teacher has some quiz or writing assignment, and whenever one of us starts to whisper we get shushed. Then, at break and lunch, it's like Dani and her friends are always nearby. And I only saw glimpses of it last week, but Dani really seems to hate Mina. Like, with a passion. She's pulling out every trick in the book. The book of *Being Mean to Someone Without Getting Detention for It* (long title, maybe).

DANI HEX'S TOP FIVE HURTFUL, BUT ULTIMATELY UNPUNISHABLE TECHNIQUES

1. The Evils. Everyone's familiar with this one. It's a long, unbroken stare of pure hatred. Often the stare–instigator's friends will join in, until a whole group of unblinking people are staring at you.
2. The Impersonal Personal Comment. This is when someone says something loudly like "Ew, what's that smell?" and then stares at their target, who definitely doesn't smell bad at all. In fact, Mina smells lightly of cocoa and strawberries, which can only be a good thing.
3. Sarcasm. A classic. She says something that's technically nice, but with a tone that makes it absolutely devastating. Like "I love your hair!" Try it.
4. Undermining. Another classic. If Mina says something and Dani hears it, she'll contradict her. Like, in physics Mina was answering a question about the phases of the moon and said, offhand, that the earth is round. Dani

put her hand up to say that it's actually not a perfect sphere, so saying it's round is incorrect. Sure, that's technically true, but oh my god, *shut up*.

5. A Ghost. If Mina ever does need to say something to Dani, like "Can you pass me that pencil?", Dani will act like she can't hear her and look around, confused, for the source of the mysterious pencil-wanting voice. This one is pretty uninspired. After seeing her other work, I actually expected better of Dani than this.

Mina acts like she doesn't even notice. Which is mature, because it makes me want to open my backpack and scream into it. It reminds me of the girls in my last school. Every time Dani and her friends look at us and laugh, it feels like history is about to repeat itself.

Wait: *maybe they know*. Maybe Dani and her cronies know what happened at my last school and they'll tell Mina, and everything will fall apart...

OK, you know what? That was very paranoid; I was being paranoid. There's no way they know anything – the gossip stream between my old inner-city school and my new tiny suburb is non-existent. Though what *is* weird is that all the same fake rumours are going around. Like the one about the boy who ate too many super-sour sweets and died. Or the kids who got murdered by a guy who'd been living in the school's air ducts for years.

After school I meet Mina at the gates.

"Finally!" I say. "Tell me about Dani's Hex and tell me now."

"Well," says Mina at the exact moment we hear a horn beep. She turns and bursts out laughing. "Unbelievable. That's my dad. I have to go. Hey, maybe I'll keep stringing you along with my thrilling backstory for ever so you have to keep hanging out with me."

"I'll hang out with you anyway, you don't have to keep me hooked with cliffhangers!" I call after her as she runs over to her dad's car.

"What's the cliffhanger? Is there a story? A scandal?"

It's Jamie. He loves gossip. In fact, it's hard to say what Jamie loves more: heists or gossip.

"I think there might be a scandal," I say as we start walking. "Basically, Mina totally seems like she'd be in the popular group, but the most popular girl, Dani Hex, hates Mina. All I know is they used to be friends and Mina says when it went bad it was a *saga*. She keeps trying to tell me about it, but we keep getting cruelly interrupted. Have you heard anything about this over at the boys' school?"

"Literally all anyone at the boys' school says about Mina and Dani is that they're hot."

"Useless."

He nods sagely. "Completely. So, secret skateboarder strikes again tomorrow morning?"

"Absolutely."

CHAPTER 4

Over the next week, life falls into a rhythm. Walking into
school with Jamie, hanging out with Mina, walking home,
telling Mum how great everything was. In the mornings,
I skate with Alex. The most we say to each other is "That
was cool" after one of us does a trick, or "You OK?"
after one of us bails. It reminds me what I like so much
about boys: the *simplicity*. Though actually, nobody is that
straightforward, not when you get to know them. Maybe
I'm idealizing Alex because Dani is working so hard to
make sure I end up with a phobia of women.

She seems to have decided that I'm hanging out with
Mina enough to have earned the right to have some of her

insults directed at me. Like when you get something free in a cafe as a loyalty reward, but in this case the reward is cruelty.

Why, why in *every school* is there a girl who dresses like an adult and says hurtful things like she gets paid for it? I'm lucky that I have a secret weapon: I'm in disguise. If Dani insults me, she's insulting the girl I pretend to be at school. So I decide not to let her bother me and, for most of the week, it works. Her comments on my hair and outfit bounce off me.

Unfortunately my low-key self-confidence means Dani just works harder to find the weak spots. On Thursday afternoon she finds one.

She's spent the whole week saying "Oh, wow, you look great, Jay!" every time she sees me. I know that looks like a compliment when it's written down, but seriously you should hear her say it (a wonderful example of Technique 3). That Thursday, as me and Mina wait outside the gates for her dad to pick her up, Dani cruises by, arm-in-arm with her friends.

"God," she says loudly, "it's so *pathetic* how she follows her around, like she's in love with her or something."

I know she's talking about me and Mina. Despite myself, I turn around, because the comment has my hackles up. I want to say something back, but I know the least convincing thing you can say when accused of having a crush is "I do not!" Then I see the look on Dani's face as she realizes she's found my weakness. I turn back to Mina, who looks anxious. God, I hope she *doesn't* think I'm some weird loser with a crush on her. But again, what can you say?

"Just so you know, I don't have a crush on you at all," I say *reassuringly.*

"Thank you, Jay," Mina says. *"Your denial is convincing and normal. If I'd ever had any suspicions that you were romantically interested in me, those are now gone."*

No, we don't say any of that. Instead, Mina says, "Sorry, Jay. I feel like I've given you the worst possible start to school. I've literally given you an enemy."

"That's OK. Somehow I don't think me and Dani would have ever hit it off."

"Well, no. Let me make it up to you, though! I can show you around town and we can get coffee or something."

"That sounds cool. I have to be honest though, I don't really like coffee."

"Oh, me neither. But there's a nice shop where you can get these ones that just taste like ice cream. They *are* expensive, but they *do* make you feel really fancy."

"Then coffee sounds great."

"Tomorrow, after school?"

"I'll check with my mum, but I think that's cool."

"Nice, that rhymed."

"Not on purpose. I would never do something like that on purpose."

Mina waves and goes over to her dad's car, and Jamie joins me. We start walking.

"Today was awesome," he starts. "Two older kids had a fight. How was your day?"

"Not bad," I say, "but Dani is truly the worst."

"What's she saying?"

"It's been low-level stuff, but just now she said I have a crush on Mina."

"Oh, that sucks," he says. There's a pause. "I mean ... do you?"

Honestly. Nobody can tell whether I'm gay or not. Not even me. I wish there was some kind of authority I could ask.

"Hi, Ms George! Before I go to English, I just wanted to check — am I gay?"

"You are! Not only that, you're destined to become a furniture designer, and the date of your death is March the 6th in the year—"

"Jay?"

On second thoughts, it's probably good teachers don't have that kind of power.

"Well, do you? Have a crush on Mina?"

"I don't know; I don't think so. What does a crush even feel like?"

"Yeah, you probably don't have a crush if you have to ask."

That's fair enough. Jamie is certainly the crush authority

out of the two of us. He's actually had a girlfriend (back in Year 7 – they held hands once, it was the talk of the town) and since then he's always had a crush going on some unattainable older girl. Meanwhile plenty of totally attainable girls at our old school would stop by my desk to ask me if my brother was single. He flirts, but he's stayed out of the dating game since Year 7.

"Great. I guess I'll just tell Dani I don't have a crush on Mina and so she should never make a joke about it again."

"That sounds convincing."

"Yeah, this is my predicament."

At dinner, Mum seems like she's in a pretty good mood. She's laughing and chatting about something her new assistant in the HR department said – it's a joke about paperwork that I don't fully understand, but I laugh too – and I hear her singing along to her music while she's cooking. I like it when she's happy like this, and I also know from experience that a mood like this is the best time to ask for something you want; what me and Jamie are allowed to do depends pretty heavily on how Mum is feeling. Like how weather affects sports, if the weather was your mother's emotions and the sport was you having a social life.

When we sit down to eat, I decide to float hanging out with Mina on Friday.

"Mum, I was wondering if it's OK if I go out after school tomorrow."

She's cutting up her chicken, but her head snaps up.

"With who?"

"With Mina. I told you about her before. She's my Buddy; she takes me to lessons and stuff."

"Oh, yes. Well, I'd probably prefer to meet her first..."

Jamie swoops in.

"Mina's great! Everyone's heard of her at the boys' school because she's basically perfect. She's pretty, she's top of all her classes, and her and Jennifer are *inseparable*. Of course I can't get a word in edgeways when they're together, they're always chatting away about mascara and straighteners and stuff."

I'm sure he's pushing it too far and almost burst out laughing, but Mum's eyes brighten up at the idea of a real girl taking me under her wing.

"That's lovely! Of course, that's fine. Lovely."

So it's settled. It's settled and it's lovely. I have a date with Mina on Friday. I mean, not like a *date*! I mean it like the saying – you know, "It's a date!" Obviously it's not a *date* date, because Mina's not gay, and possibly neither am I. It's just two school friends being friends after school. Which is normal, and not something to be anxious about.

I'm so anxious about it. What if I can't think of anything to say? Yes, we talk all day at school, Monday to Friday, but maybe things will be different after three-thirty. And what if I *do* have a crush on her? What if I've made a good friend, and I ruin it because I want her to be my girlfriend?

What if I have a crush on her, and she notices and thinks I'm weird? Honestly. Not knowing your sexuality is a constant nightmare.

At least I can go skateboarding in the morning to clear my head.

Alex is already there when I get to the skatepark, but he's not skating. He's just sitting with his legs hanging off the edge of a ramp, gazing into the middle distance.

"Hey, man," I say as I roll past.

"Hey."

He's still gazing away thoughtfully, so I decide not to bother him. After all, I've got my own things to be thoughtful about ... even though I'm choosing to focus on doing kickflips instead.

Then Alex sighs loudly. I glance over at him, but he's still gazing away. I keep skating. When he sighs a second time, I figure I have to say something.

"You OK?"

He looks at me like he's just noticed me there. "Yeah."

I stay still for a minute, then start to skate again.

"It's just..."

I stop skating.

"I don't know. Do you ever feel like other people don't really get you?"

"Yes," I say too quickly. "Um – are you thinking about anybody in particular?"

"Everybody, I guess. But also my dad."

"What's he like?"

"He doesn't get me."

I feel like we're going in circles here. "How so?"

"He hates that I skate. Like your mum, I guess."

Note to self: choose a religion for my imaginary mother.

"Does he try to stop you?"

"Not really. He just lets me know how disappointed he is. It's always like, *You're athletic, why don't you play real sports? Why don't you have a girlfriend yet?*"

I never expected Alex to tell me anything so personal. It sort of breaks the rules of a skatepark acquaintanceship. I sit down on my board awkwardly.

"That sounds hard."

"Yeah. We're so different."

"He probably feels like you don't get him too," I say, thinking about Mum. I know how it feels to be the polar opposite of the person you're meant to be most like. Especially when I was little, Mum would always talk about how me and Jamie were the kids, but me and her were "the girls". A team. As I got older and it became clear I wasn't exactly "the girls", she stopped saying that stuff so much. Ever since we moved, I feel like she thinks of us as a team again … but it feels fake to me. We're just not the same like that. I don't think we're even similar.

"That's true. But I can't be like he wants me to be. I wish he'd understand that."

"Have you ever said that to him?"

"No. I don't really have anybody to talk to about this stuff."

I smile. "You're talking to me."

"That's true," he says. He smiles back. "Anyway. Bet you can't kickflip the funbox first try."

"I will absolutely bet you I *can*," I say, getting up and back on to my board.

It's kind of sketchy, but I totally land it. Nothing like gambling to keep you motivated.

Alex cheers. "That was sick!"

I roll up to join him at the top of the ramp and give a little bow. He suddenly grabs my fist and pulls me into one of those bro hugs. You know the ones, when two guys hold their clenched fists in between their bodies and then crash into them with their chests. For a second I feel his arm press against me, and his other hand lightly brushes my hip.

"You know, Jay," he says, "it's cool to have another real skater in town."

He holds on to my hand for another second and smiles at me. His eyes are really warm and dark and his hair is falling into them and he smells very nice. He takes off down the ramp and I feel like I've had all the breath knocked out of me and like all my skin is tingling.

Oh god. Oh no.

So *that's* a crush.

CHAPTER 5

"How was your skate?" Jamie asks cheerfully as we start walking to school later that morning.

"Fine!" I say, significantly too loud. He jumps.

"What happened?"

"Nothing happened."

"You sound like something happened."

"Nope. This isn't how I sound when something's happened."

"You're all loud and high-pitched."

"I don't think that's how I sound!!" I say, loud and high-pitched.

He looks at me suspiciously. "Are you nervous about hanging out with Mina after school?"

Thank god! That sounds completely reasonable. "That's exactly it, Jamie. You're extremely insightful."

"You shouldn't worry at all! You just have to be yourself. The right people will like you for who you are..." Jamie launches into an encouraging speech. I nod, but I'm not listening. I'm not going to tell him about my sudden and baffling crush on Alex because I don't want anyone to know about it EVER, but I do try to imagine the advice he'd give if I did.

Jamie would go into full strategy mode. *"So you've developed a crush on Alex,"* he'd say, *stroking his handlebar moustache and polishing one of the many awards pinned to his general's uniform as he paces the war room.* *"An unexpected twist. But not, I think, a cause for concern."*

"Really? Because I'm concerned."

"Think about it this way. Nothing on the outside has actually changed. Your feelings have changed on the inside, but only you know that. You're not going to tell him how you feel, are you?"

"No! I'm not even telling the real you how I feel."

Jamie starts drawing complicated maps on the blackboard behind him. *"Exactly. Now tell me, do you really think there is any world or parallel universe where Alex, the whole world's crush, would like you back?"*

"That's quite mean. But no."

"Exactly. You just make sure you keep your little crush a secret,

and the two of you can keep up your skatepark acquaintanceship. The only thing that could go wrong is if you lose it completely and decide to start telling people your feelings."

Both of us laugh merrily and clink our glasses of whisky together.

Real Jamie is finishing up his real speech, which I have completely missed.

"... don't you think?" he says, wrapping up.

"Jamie, you're a genius and you're right about everything." He *is* right – or the Jamie in my imagination is, at any rate. So long as I don't let anything slip – and I'm good at keeping secrets – what does it matter if I keep thinking about Alex's slow, sad smile and strong arms? Nobody else has to know that. Truly I hope that nobody ever does.

I bounce into school feeling positive. Sure, I'm still nervous about hanging out with Mina, but now I have a much bigger anxiety to overshadow that one. I feel like I've cracked a code. If you're scared about something, just find something scarier to worry about. In my case, I was worried that I might be gay and would accidentally ruin a friendship. So instead what I've done is develop a secret identity and an even more stressful crush. Ta-da!

OK, when I put it like that it doesn't sound like I'm in a great position, but still: positivity.

I manage to *stay* positive all morning, even though I'm wearing The Skirt, which always removes some pep from my step. I even start to feel kind of excited about going out with Mina. When I sit down next to her in class, she starts chanting "coffee friends, coffee friends", so we both quietly chant that for a little while. In the hall we pass Dani, but I pretend that I simply can't see her and daintily step far enough around her that I can't hear what I'm sure is a witty but hurtful comment.

But of course, I'd almost forgotten that today is Friday and I said I'd have a "little chat" with Hugo after PE. You can't win 'em all.

When PE is over, I get changed and awkwardly stay behind in the gym. Hugo beams and waves me over to sit on a bench opposite the one he's already sprawled over in what I imagine he thinks is a fun, chill *I'm-a-cool-teacher* position.

"Jennifer! Let's crack on!"

Yeah. *Let's crack on.* What Hugo doesn't know is that I have a plan to make sure he never wants to have another one of these talks ever again.

JAY'S TOP FIVE TIPS FOR RUINING A CONVERSATION WITH AN ADULT

1. Unnecessary formality. For example, when they ask how you are, say, "I'm very well, thank you very much. And how are *you*

today?" This makes it clear that you're not going to be "letting them in".

2. Answering questions with questions. E.g. "How is school?" gets answered by "How is work?"
3. One-word answers. Everything is "good", "fine" or "great".
4. Loss of focus. Just zone right out. Stare at the clock. Read the fire safety sign on the wall.
5. Give off an atmosphere of total zen. You are untouchable. You're like a Buddhist monk, meditating in the middle of a storm or something. It would probably be good if you were like this in the rest of your life, instead of only cultivating inner peace for spite.

I'm aware this completely defeats the point of agreeing to these heart-to-hearts with Hugo. But I can't emphasize enough how much I've hated him from the moment I saw him. And how much I *hate* being called Jennifer.

"How are you today?"

"I'm very well, Hugo, thank you for asking. Yourself?"

At first he looks pleased. "I'm great, thanks. So how's the school week been?"

"Fantastic."

There's a long pause.

"Yeah? That's good. What's been going on?"

"Plenty."

Another pause. I can feel he's trying to wait me out so I have to talk to fill the silence. He's underestimating my patience.

"Are you finding it OK making friends?"

"Yes, thanks," I say, looking dreamily out of the window.

"Something interesting going on out there?" he tries.

"No," I say, in the same whimsical tone.

Out of the corner of my eye I can see his jaw starting to tighten.

"Something I thought we could discuss today," he says, "is that arm of yours. How it ended up getting broken."

It takes a pretty enormous effort not to flinch. But I know he's trying to get a reaction, so I maintain my air of sarcastic detachment. *Nice try, Hugo.*

"Oh, yes. A tragic accident."

"It doesn't sound like it was an accident to me," he says, pulling my file out of his bag and flicking through it.

That's it. Time to check out entirely.

I spend the rest of the session reading all the titles of the posters on the wall and trying to memorize the order of them. Hugo gets angrier and angrier, although he keeps his voice calm. Some of what he says gets through.

Do I understand why the kids at my old school might have found me confusing or strange? Do I understand why they might have felt I was trying to trick or deceive them with the way I dressed? Can I see how much more comfortable the people around me are now that I'm not trying to be different? Don't I understand that he's *just here to help*?

I say nothing.

Near the end of the session, he snaps. "Do you realize, Jennifer, that you're wasting your time and mine?"

I look at the clock. One minute to go.

"We meet for an hour, Hugo," I say philosophically and very annoyingly. "No matter how we spend that time, an hour passes anyway. And that's the hour! I'll see you next time."

Hugo's face is bright red, and he looks like he would punch me if that wasn't illegal.

Mission accomplished.

I open the door and jump. Ms George is standing right outside. She looks from furious Hugo to me, a dark expression on her face. I can't tell who's in trouble, me or him.

"Have you been standing there this whole time?" I ask nervously.

"No," she says, putting a hand on my shoulder and marching me away without saying anything to Hugo, "just for a few minutes. I thought I'd walk you to your next class."

"Thanks," I say calmly, twisting my shirt in my hands not-calmly.

"Let's step in here for a second," she says, steering me into her classroom. Yeah, I'm definitely in trouble. She closes the door.

"I saw Mina alone in the cafeteria and she said you're doing academic 'catch-up' sessions with Hugo. I thought I'd bring you a sandwich." She's holding a ham and cheese sandwich, which is very sweet of her, but also gripping it slightly too hard. She must be angry about how she heard me speaking to Hugo.

"I guess they're more like little chats to see how I'm settling in."

"Mm–hm. And how are you getting on with Hugo?"

"Um…" What's the point in lying? I'm pretty sure she heard at least some of what just happened. "Not that well."

"I didn't think so. Have you told your mother that?"

"Uh…"

"You're under no obligation to attend these meetings. Why don't you just tell your mother you don't want to speak to him?"

I think that's an *absurd idea*. Ms George has no idea what she's dealing with.

"I could do it, if you wanted?"

That actually might be even worse than her first idea. I can just picture Mum's face if she even heard Ms George call me Jay.

"Jay?" Mum would gasp. "You dare call her JAY? YOU DARE?"

70

She stands up to her full sixty metres and grabs a circling helicopter out of the sky. Ms George and I start to run, but Mum chases us, crushing cars beneath her tasteful ankle boots. She draws back her arm and throws the helicopter. Ms George and I scream, diving behind a building—

Who am I kidding? Mum's one metre sixty, and she wouldn't get angry like that, she'd just start to cry, and she'd probably ask me why I want to change back to how I used to be when we finally have something in common...

"Jay?"

"I'm sorry, Ms George," I say awkwardly, "but we can't do that."

Ms George is quiet for a moment. She also looks kind of like she wants to punch something. I'm having that effect on adults today.

"OK," she says, "but I have another idea. How do you feel about staying behind for an hour on Mondays to talk to *me*?"

"Am I in trouble?"

"Not at all. We can talk about schoolwork, or whatever you like. What do you think?"

I'm suspicious. Why would a teacher want to spend time with me unless I was in trouble? But I like Ms George. She seems cool, even though she really has that sandwich in a chokehold. Still, I think it's not me who she's angry at.

"OK."

"Good. You'd better get to class. See you later, Jay."

She hands me the crushed sandwich. I leave the classroom. I'm not entirely sure what's just happened.

"Coffee friend!" Mina says cheerfully when I slide into my seat. "How was your horribly boring session thing?"

"Horribly boring. *And* I have to do another one on Mondays after school now."

Between my double life and hanging out with all these teachers, my schedule is really filling up.

"That can't be legal. How much work do you need to catch up on anyway? Didn't they teach you anything in your old school?"

"No," I say, "I really don't come to school to learn, I'm just a big fan of whiteboards and they're hard to find anywhere else."

I say it like I'm completely serious, but I can't keep a straight face for long and we both start giggling.

"Don't get too excited, but there's one in the room right now."

"I know, I'm trying not to scream."

At the end of the day, we join everybody milling around outside. I can't help looking for *him*. Just when I'm giving up hope, I hear wheels on concrete. I try to look around casually, but I don't think I manage it.

Alex is doing that thing again where he tries to take off his tie and stuff it in his backpack, all while skating.

72

I wonder if he's still thinking about our conversation this morning. I wonder if he's going back to the skatepark. I wish I could go with him, and just, like, talk to him some more, you know? I don't really know him at all. Maybe I don't even have a crush on him. I just think about him a lot and get really excited when I might see him. And blush for no reason.

"Jay?"

I turn around and see Mina with her eyebrows raised.

"What?"

"What was that?"

"Nothing. What was … you?"

"Uh-huh. You practically spun around as soon as you heard his skateboard."

Great. Mina definitely knows about my not-crush. Girls are too perceptive. Another reason they're scary. She links arms with me and we start walking.

"You're gonna have to tell me *all* about that over coffee."

CHAPTER 6

OK, so actually it turns out that hanging out with Mina after school is exactly the same as hanging out with her in school, only we're in a coffee shop instead of geography. She's just as funny and we get on just as well; we're talking so fast that I start to think she might have forgotten about catching me gazing longingly at Alex. But of *course* she hasn't.

"So. Why were you staring at skater boy?"

"Was I? I hadn't noticed."

"Jay. Come on. If you'd spun around any faster, you would've been breakdancing."

Well. Deception isn't going to work on Mina.

"I guess I was looking at him."

"Why?"

"Um … well, because … uh…"

"Jay, it's OK. I know why you were staring."

"Oh."

"And I think it's really cool."

"You — you do?"

"Yeah, obviously! I don't know why you're embarrassed about it. You don't need to be."

I feel like I haven't blinked in a long time. We stare at each other for a long few seconds while I try to work out what's happening. Can Mina read minds? Is she all-knowing? What do you say to that?

Thanks for supporting my crush! Just make sure you never tell anyone about it, especially not Alex, because he *might not think my religion allows that.*

"It's awesome that you skate!" Mina spells it out.

She still might be a mind reader, but at least I didn't say the other thing.

"Your brother said you skateboard the first time I met him, remember? Then you both panicked and tried to pretend he hadn't said it. It was really weird."

"Oh… OH. Right. Yes." On balance, this is an easier secret to reveal. "I do skate, yeah."

"That's cool. I know loads of girls must do it, but can you believe I've never actually met a girl who skateboards before?"

"Yeah, I've only ever met one or two." It's like Mina says: I know a lot of girls must skate, because there are women who are pro skaters, but I never met any girls who were seriously into it at my last skatepark.

"Is that why you were embarrassed about it? 'Cause it's mostly, like, a guy thing?"

"Yeah, exactly."

"Well, you really shouldn't be. It's unfair that anyone would think someone shouldn't do something just because they're not a boy, right?"

"You're so right."

"I always am. And, in the nicest possible way, who would care that you like to skate?"

"Yeah, you're right!" I say again. Because you know what? She totally is. Why *should* anyone care about my hobbies?

And then I almost choke on my coffee milkshake. Mum is walking into the shop and looking around. I should have lied and said I wouldn't be in town.

"Mina," I say, talking fast, "don't call me Jay."

"What?"

"Just for the next five minutes, please don't call me Jay. Or mention the skate—"

"Jennifer!"

Mina turns around and sees Mum swooping down on us. Though Mina probably doesn't assume she's my mum because we look so different. Mum's wearing a different sweater dress thing this time, and bright red lipstick. She smells powerfully of rose water. For all Mina knows we're being accosted by a very floral, very dangerous stranger. She shoots me a nervous look.

"Hi, Mum," I say, trying not to sound too filled with dread.

"I was just on my way to meet Carly to get our nails done, when I saw you both and thought I'd say hi!"

It's a lie. I know it's a lie. She was looking for me.

"You must be Mina," she says. "I've heard so much about you!"

It's amazing how fast Mina can turn on the charm. She shoots me one *we'll talk about this later* look and then doesn't miss a beat as she says, "And you must be Jennifer's mum! I hope you've only heard good things!"

The next second they're chatting away like a pair of adults. Mina asks Mum if she's getting her nails long or short (which is weird – how could you make nails longer?) and says something confident about "French tips", which practically makes Mum glow. I look down at my short, chewed-up nails, immediately bored by the conversation, which is a good sign – if I'm bored, Mum is usually having a great time.

"You know what, why don't you girls come along and have your nails done too? My treat!"

Mina clearly catches the colour draining from my face because she says, "Oh my goodness, I would absolutely *love* to, but I promised my mum I'd go with her this Sunday. She'd be so sad if we didn't get them done together."

"Of course," says Mum, and I can see her getting a bit misty. For a second I'm scared we might witness a full Sad Mum explosion. I know she's imagining a world where I'm going with her to get my nails done, and we're the ones talking about French tips, and I actually know what French tips *are*. (I'd like to think they're advice about, like, where to go for lunch in Paris. But I'm pretty sure that's not it).

It makes me sad too. Why *can't* I be the daughter she wishes she had? Why *don't* I want pretty French nails? "I'll see you at home, Jennifer. Mina, it's been so lovely to meet you. Come around for dinner any time."

"I'd love to! It's such a pleasure to finally meet you."

Mum takes her leave, and I spend about ten seconds trying to avoid making eye contact with Mina, whose eyebrows are practically running away into her hair.

"How about those French tips, huh?" I say, conversationally.

"Uh-uh. You're gonna have to tell me what was going on there, Jay."

"Well, Mina," I say, *"the fact is that I've deceived you."*

The cafe is suddenly a fancy bar, and everything is in black and white. Mina is smoking a cigarette in one of those holder things.

"I'm not who I appear to be at all." I shrug off my mink coat

to reveal a suit. *"The fact is, I'm not a proper girl, I'm a weird …* thing *that likes menswear and skateboarding."*

"Lord knows you aren't the first man to lie to me," she'd say, blowing a smoke ring and smoothing down the skirt of her red ballgown (I know I said everything is black and white, but you'd somehow know the dress was red), and—

"Jay."

I take a deep breath. "My mum just has a bit of a problem with things that she thinks are, like, boyish. With regards to me."

"And that includes skateboarding and being called Jay."

"Those are probably top of the list."

"No wonder you're so weird about skateboarding."

"I wouldn't say I'm weird."

"Of course *you* wouldn't. I've got to say, you're starting to make a lot more sense."

"I am?"

"Yeah. You're actually, like, a skater girl, tomboy type. That's why you don't know how to roll up a school skirt."

She's wrong and she's right. I can see the image Mina has in her head right now, of the girl she thinks I want to be: ripped jeans, maybe a tight T-shirt with a band logo on it, long surfer-girl hair, gracefully riding a longboard down a hill. Maybe she wears a little bit of mascara, but mostly says she "can't be bothered with make-up". Boys love her, because she's still pretty but also has some of the

79

same interests as them. Maybe she plays video games with them, or is willing to competitively chug fizzy drinks, or likes that band they think only other boys like.

Mina's off the mark. But she's a bit closer to knowing me now, at least.

"Yeah, I definitely still don't know how to roll up a school skirt. Even though you've shown me."

"You'll get there, young one," she says. "So tell me something about where you used to live. You never talk about it."

"It was … much busier than here."

"I had sort of guessed that our nation's capital would be. What were your friends like?"

"Mostly boys. We skated together, that kind of thing."

"Oooh, did you leave a boyfriend behind?"

I laugh. "No, no. They were just friends."

"Do you still talk?"

"Not really, since I don't have a phone any more."

"Whoa. *You don't have a phone?!* You don't have TikTok? Instagram? Twitter? Snapchat? Wait, do you just have *Facebook*, or something shameful like that?"

"No."

She stares at me. "Are you Amish?"

Huh. Maybe I should tell Alex I'm Amish. Actually, no, I probably wouldn't have access to a skateboard if I were Amish. I'd probably be farming.

"No. Mum was just really strict about social media,

so I didn't get a phone until I was fourteen. And then I broke it skating and she didn't want to buy me a new one."

"Wait. Are you actually running away from some sort of dark past?"

"Oh, yeah. You got me. Nothing major, obviously, just armed robbery, that kind of thing."

"Banks?"

"Mostly banks, yeah."

"Well, there's only one bank in town and far fewer people, so you might find this one harder to get away with."

"I like a challenge. Worst comes to worst I'll just have to move to a new town and get a new Buddy to show me around."

"Unfortunately they would never be as smart, beautiful or talented as me. I just want you to be prepared for that disappointment."

"I'll keep that in mind before I return to a life of crime. Anyway, you just asked me *so* many questions. Is it my turn?"

"You get two questions. That's my best offer."

"Fine."

I kind of can't believe how much fun talking to Mina is. It always feels like she's teasing me, but in a nice way. It's, like, warm but also exciting. Who knew? The power of friendship, huh?

"OK, question one. You said Alex isn't your type. Who is?"

"Oooh, straight in at the deep end, OK!"

Uh-oh. Why did I ask her that? It was just the first thing that came to mind. I'm ready to panic, but then Mina grins at me.

"Someone with more of a sense of humour than him, definitely."

At first I want to stand up for him. Alex is funny. Not that I've ever heard him *be* funny, but I'm sure he is. Then I remember that, as far as Mina's aware, I've never spoken to the guy.

"And more down to earth," she continues. "He seems kind of stuck up. He never really talks to anyone, even though girls are always trying to get his attention. Dani has a *huge* thing for him."

That's interesting information.

"He is pretty good-looking, I guess."

"Yeah, but in kind of a boring, obvious way, you know?"

I nod sagely, but I'm thinking, *What's wrong with being obviously good-looking?* Isn't that what everybody actually likes? Surely nobody wants to have to look at someone for twenty minutes to work out if they fancy them? Except Mina, apparently.

"All right then, question two. What are your parents like?"

Mina snorts and almost spills some coffee, laughing. "I didn't see that coming!"

"Oh, sorry; you don't have to answer."

"No, it's totally fine, the crushes-to-parents transition just threw me off. I'll give you the full run-down. So my dad does some kind of finance job. He's always wearing a suit. And he's so sweet … like, he still offers to read me bedtime stories every night. He has the best voice, really deep, with a Nigerian accent. My mum is American and she's always wearing lipstick and heels. Seriously glamorous. We're close. She's easy to talk to, like she'll see a stranger and within five seconds they'll have in-jokes. And she's smart; she goes around teaching sociology at different universities."

I swallow. The way she talks about her parents – it's nice. You can tell she really likes them. She almost talks about them like they're her friends, which I just can't imagine feeling about Mum.

"I feel like I just talked a lot," says Mina. "Was that more information than you wanted?"

"Not at all! That was exactly the right amount. I mean if you'd said any more, I would have got bored, but…"

"Oh, shut up," she says, grinning. "Can I ask you more questions?"

"You can ask *one* more. You've had loads."

"Well, I know about your mum. What's your dad like?"

"I don't really know him that well."

"Oh."

"It's OK, people always think it's a bigger deal than it is. Him and my mum broke up just before I was born. We used to see him when we were younger, but never that often. When I was seven he moved to Canada for work, and we just talked less and less."

"Do you look like him?"

"Kind of. Why?"

"You don't really look like your mum. Except your eyes. You have really nice eyes, by the way."

I'm blushing. I scramble around for something to say. "Hey, can you finally tell me the Dani story?"

Mina hesitates, and maybe I'm imagining it, but I think she looks nervous. "Monday? I've gotta head off if I'm going to be back for dinner," she says. "And not to sound like a total loser, but this was really fun. We should keep up the trend of hanging out both in and out of school."

"I'd like to keep up that trend. It's a cool trend. It's trendy."

Stop talking.

"I'll see you on Monday!" she says. "Do we hug?"

"We could hug," I say, hoping I'm not about to be too horribly awkward. I know how to hug a boy; you just sort of crash your bodies into each other and hit each other on the back. What do you do to a girl while you're hugging? Pat her?

84

I go for a gentle shoulder pat as she wraps her arms briefly around my waist.

"Did you just pat me on the back?"

"Yes, but only as a treat. Don't expect that every time."

She bursts out laughing. Thank god.

"See you later, weirdo."

I'm in a really good mood when I enter the house. Jamie tackles me from the side as soon as I walk in.

"Ahhhh!"

"How was your date?" he asks, making kissy noises at me.

"Oh, shut up. It wasn't a date. But it was really nice and went very well."

"Way to go, champ."

"Jennifer!" I hear Mum call from the living room.

"Are we at risk of Sad Mum this evening?" I whisper.

"Nope. Spirits are good."

I slip into the living room where Mum is reading a book, turning the pages carefully with her freshly painted nails. She positively beams at me.

"How was the rest of your girl time?"

"It was great," I say, sliding into a chair. "What did you think of Mina?"

"Oh, she is just a darling. And so put together and pretty!"

"Yes."

"It's a shame you couldn't come and get your nails done with me."

"Yes. Yours look really nice, though."

"Do you think so?" She holds them up to the light. They look like normal nails to me, but a bit longer and shinier.

I decide to take a swing. "Oh, French tips?"

She looks shocked. "Wow, that Mina's rubbing off on you."

"Oh, yeah, she knows so much about make-up and stuff. She's even said she'll give me a makeover." This isn't true, but sometimes it's just easier to say things Mum will like. And you know what? She looks so happy it makes me feel happy too.

"Make sure to send me some pictures when she does. And speaking of pictures…" – she reaches into her handbag, hanging off the edge of the sofa – "I think it did you a lot of good to take a little technology break. But you're settling in so well, and you've clearly made such a good friend, so I've got you a new phone!"

She hands it to me. I'll be honest, it doesn't look state of the art, but I'm really excited to have a phone again.

"It's the same as Jamie's, just for texts and calls; you can't go online," she says quickly, "but you can message your friends and take pictures. What more do you need?"

"What more *do* you need?" I repeat pointlessly, thinking this will probably make me look even more Amish than not having a phone at all. But that night when I go to bed, having it on my bedside table makes me feel just a bit more independent. Like, I could text anybody I wanted to, and Mum wouldn't have to know. Sure, I'll have to get someone's number first. But still. It's a start.

CHAPTER 7

I'm actually kind of excited to get to school, which is weird. Nobody should look forward to Monday. But Mina's promised to tell me the rest of the Dani Hex saga and I'm a sucker for a cliffhanger. Maybe we should use cliffhangers to make ourselves do everything. Don't want to get an injection? Just make your doctor tell you half of a secret first.

"I'm sorry, doctor, I can't do it," I say, backing rapidly away from his needle and pushing a chair in between us.

"Oh," he says sadly, "but afterwards I was going to tell you … about the amulet. You know what, never mind."

He starts to pack his doctor tools away, but I hesitate.

"Hang on, what were you going to tell me?"

"It's nothing."

"It doesn't sound like nothing."

Next thing you know I'm merrily getting a flu jab while my doctor tells me about the cursed amulet his grandmother has passed down to him.

In Ms George's class I take my seat next to Mina.

"Morning!" she says, perkily. "Good weekend? Did ya miss me?"

"Of course. I wrote you several letters and nearly died from the heartache."

"I thought so."

"Can I finally hear the Dani story?"

"Good morning!" Ms George says, popping out from behind her desk. Yet another interruption. Mina dramatically raises her hands towards heaven. She keeps making silly faces, so I totally miss Ms George's morning pep talk from trying not to laugh.

I snap back to attention as she says, "Mina, Jay, could you stay back a minute?"

We wait for everyone else to file out.

"Did we do something wrong?" I ask nervously.

"Of course not!" Ms George says, laughing. "You're both model students, don't be silly." She's absolutely talking more about Mina there. I'm probably just around Mina enough that Ms George has assumed I'm also academic and helpful. "I actually wanted to ask you something, Mina.

Planning Committee meetings are starting next week, and you're still signed up as treasurer and Dani's told me they don't have anyone else willing to take over…"

What's the Planning Committee?

Mina's face falls instantly. "I was *not* planning to stay on the Planning Committee," she says. "The Planning Committee led by Dani. And filled with all her friends."

Ah.

"I have noticed you two aren't as inseparable as you used to be," says Ms George. I raise my eyebrows at Mina. I *really* need this backstory. "But the committee really needs someone in charge of the budget to stop the whole Summer Dance falling apart."

"They're already starting to plan the Summer Dance?" I say in disbelief. How much planning can a dance even take? Put people in a room. Make them dance.

"Students take the Summer Dance pretty seriously at Heath," Ms George says, "and it's just one meeting per term. I know you and Dani aren't as close as you used to be, but I think that working together on this might be a good way to rebuild that bridge. I know she's difficult, but you two have fallen out and made up before! You're a good influence on her, and she values your friendship."

I catch Mina's eye for a second and can immediately see that Ms George is missing the point. She's doing that thing teachers do where they convince themselves that even mean kids have a good heart really, and that putting nicer kids in groups with them will influence them for the better rather than just giving them target practice. Do teachers *remember* being teenagers?

"I don't know…" Mina says. It's the first time I've seen her unsure of herself.

"It's only one meeting per term. And I was thinking that Jay could go along with you," Ms George says soothingly.

"Of course I can," I say quickly, because I don't want Mina to be left alone in there.

Ms George beams. She looks happy — so naive, like there's no evil in the world.

Mina looks like she wants to say no but is having trouble rejecting an innocent.

"*Fine*," she finally says. "Let's go, Jay."

I nod awkwardly at Ms George as I chase off after Mina. In the hall, she grabs my arm and hustles me into the bathroom. She pushes each of the stall doors to make sure we're alone.

"How is Dani the leader of the Planning Committee?" I ask. "Shouldn't it be a final-year?"

"You'd be amazed what you can accomplish when you're blonde and cruel. Looks like I have to fill you in on the Dani Hex Saga straight away."

"Finally!" I say, hopping up to sit on a sink.

"So, Dani and I became best friends when we were three."

"Wow! Was she always this mean?"

"Actually, yes. But I think me being her best friend made her nicer, to be honest. At least when she said something horribly cutting, I was there to make it sound like a joke. I thought it *was* a joke, and she just had a mean sense of humour. And she *is* really funny, so that confused things. But I think she's kind of mean above all. We did everything together, up until a month ago."

I'm already excited to tell Jamie about this. He *loves* drama, even about people he barely knows.

"We went to a party together. Someone had stolen a bunch of vodka from their parents, and we all got kinda drunk."

I nod in a *I-know-how-it-is* way and do not mention that my one drinking experience was when Jamie and I shared a six pack of beer somebody's older brother sold him. We didn't feel any different afterwards, and then realized it was alcohol-free and he'd been totally ripped off. He still gets embarrassed if I bring it up.

"Then Dani and I..." She pauses for a split second. "We had a fight."

"What about?"

"I don't even remember," she says. She doesn't meet my eye. "Must not really have been that important. But it was big at the time. She hates me now. As you've seen."

"Seriously? Because of one fight?"

"Yes."

"Like … one fight? That you don't remember?"

"Yes."

"No details?"

"You look disappointed."

"I was just expecting a little more drama and intrigue, I guess."

More than that, I have a weird feeling that Mina's not telling me something. But why wouldn't she?

"We always had a volatile friendship."

"Good word."

"Thank you. But this time is different. She clearly doesn't want to make up, and now neither do I. But it's a good thing. It made me realize that Dani's not a nice person and she's definitely not a good friend. I was always making excuses for the way she would undermine me and talk about me behind my back. Like, *you're* nicer and a better friend to me already than she ever was."

We're standing on a beautiful cliff at sunset. "Then I guess we should make it official," I say, getting down on one knee and producing a friendship bracelet from the inside pocket of my tuxedo. "Can I be your new best friend?"

"Oh, Jay!" Mina gasps, jumping with delight. "Of course you can! Of course you are!"

I tie the bracelet around her wrist, and—

"And of *course* she leads the Planning Committee. I get that Ms George thinks we've just had some silly disagreement we need to work through, but Dani is going to make this so horrible – for me, and probably for you too. I'm really sorry."

I don't mind at all. I'm still high off Mina confirming that what we're doing is a real live friendship. "It's not your fault at all."

She smiles. "Thanks. You know, Jay, I'm so glad we met. When I signed up to be the new kid's Buddy, I hoped you'd be nice, but I had no idea you'd be this cool. At least if we're in this committee together, we can laugh about it!"

I don't say anything, I just beam at her. We step out of the bathroom and I feel invincible.

Of course, that's the moment that Dani passes by with her gang.

"Oh look," she says loudly, "the girls who had to beg Ms George to get them on the committee."

Ah. Ms George has told her. Great. Mina and I can laugh about this later, like she said.

Dani locks her blue eyes on to me. "You know the Planning Committee has to pick the dress code for the dance, right? So you … have to know how to dress?"

Her gang laughs, and they all sweep away down the hallway. I look at Mina with my mouth hanging open. I'm practically winded. Dani's putdowns are so well *crafted*. And so perfectly *delivered*.

"Yeah," Mina says, patting me on the back. "Well, maybe we'll be able to laugh about it with hindsight. Like, in a few years."

CHAPTER 8

When the bell for the end of the day rings, I head to Ms George's classroom for my session with her. Have you ever been in school after everybody else has left? It's so weird. Like, you go there pretty much every day, but it looks like a horror movie set two seconds after the last bell.

Or maybe that's my nerves talking. I'm still not sure if I'm in trouble or not for the way I was with Hugo last Friday. I know Ms George said I wasn't, but adults sometimes *say* you're not in trouble and then it turns out you actually are. If they *do* say you're in trouble, that really means you're in, like, *so much trouble*. Basically, you can't trust them.

I knock, and Ms George calls for me to come in. The room is only lit by a lamp, so her desk looks like it's floating in a warm circle of light surrounded by gloom. She pushes her curly dark hair back and I notice she has some subtle blonde streaks in it and that her cheeks dimple when she smiles. She seems so warm and friendly that I'm instantly smiling back. The radio is playing quietly and there are two cans of Fanta out on the desk. I slide into the seat across the desk from her and she pushes one of the Fantas towards me.

"Do you believe you're not in trouble now?"

"Uh … well, you said I'm not."

"I did. Because you're not. But you clearly didn't believe me."

"No, but I do now. Because of the Fanta."

"You don't give enemies Fanta. Jay, I feel like I haven't taken enough time to get to know you. It's hard with twenty other kids in the room. How are your classes? You like history, don't you?"

"Yeah, I do. I don't know if I'm that good at it in a 'school' way, but I like watching old movies and documentaries and stuff. I like the way stuff used to look."

"Me too. What do you like about it?"

"I guess I just like imagining all the different ways the world has been. Or could be."

"What a lovely way to put it."

"Oh, well, thanks."

This is actually … *nice*. It's weird to have a nice time with an adult. I usually think that if someone's over sort of twenty-five (is that when people turn into adults and get loads of kids and jobs and stuff?) any conversation with them will be at best boring and at worst awful. But this feels like a conversation I could have with a friend. Ms George is much smarter and more sensible than any of my friends, but you get the idea. I'm still nervous, though. Call it anxiety, but I keep having a weird image of her yelling "Ha! Tricked you! You're in serious trouble!" and throwing the desk at me or something.

But instead she just keeps asking questions about my life. I talk about how great Mina is and how much fun it is being friends with her. I tell her about Jamie too, and how he always looks out for me and makes me laugh. She tells me about her brother, Marcus, who sends her pictures of his cat every day. She shows me one where Marcus has balanced a cap on its head, which is delightful to both of us even if the cat doesn't look thrilled. It's fun.

"OK, look," she says as the end of the hour starts to approach, "I'll be completely honest with you here. I'm not sure I like that Hugo guy."

"I didn't know teachers were allowed to not like other teachers."

"I'll let you in on a secret – we actually don't even have to like the students. But it's my impression that you feel uncomfortable around Hugo. I'm wondering why that is."

I like Ms George, but I'm not sure I can really give her a full answer to that.

"Well, to keep things brief," I'd say, *" for the last few months, since a traumatic event at my old school that I don't think there's any need to go into, I've finally given in to my mother's lifelong pressure to dress like a girl. If I'm honest, I would say the pressure has been getting to me, which is maybe causing me to act out a bit. Nothing dramatic, I've just started a double life. But I digress. The reason I don't like Hugo is that he feels like a spy sent by my mother to make sure I'm not harbouring any secret desires to dress like my real self again. Does that sound paranoid? Maybe I'm just a little anxious because I now live in constant fear of someone discovering who I really am. But what do I know? Maybe you can ask Hugo; I'm sure he's worked out a full psychological profile of me from our LITTLE CHATS."*

I opt for the easier answer (AKA, the lie).

"He's fine. Mum wants me to have regular meetings with him to settle in, and it's only once a week."

Ms George frowns. It doesn't look like she believes me.

"We could tell your mother if you'd rather not meet with him?"

"No, really! It's fine." The last thing I want is to give Mum any reason to think I'm not playing by the rules.

"It's great you're settling in so well otherwise, though."

I kind of wish people would stop saying "settling in". It makes me feel like a bird in a nest.

"I think the Planning Committee will be a good chance

for you to get to know more of the girls too. And don't worry about Dani; she and Mina always work things out."

I smile and nod and try to ignore the burst of jealousy I feel when she says that.

Wait, why do I feel jealous? Mina is totally allowed to have another, more evil best friend if she wants to.

When I walk out of the school gates and head home I find my new phone is blowing up with texts from Mum, all of them demanding to know where I am. Oh no: I forgot to tell her I'd be late!

I rush back to the house. Jamie meets me at the door but can't say anything because Mum is staring straight at us, so he just gives an eyebrow raise of warning.

"Hi, Mum!" I say, with as much enthusiasm as I can. She's sitting on the couch and her eyes are wide with panic. The trick here is to get your words in fast. "I'm so so sorry that I didn't text you! I stayed behind for Homework Club."

There's a pause while she stares at me. I stare back. Jamie stares at both of us. I can hear the clock ticking. Then she breathes out.

"That's good. Jamie said you were probably at Homework Club. Just make sure you tell me next time."

I exhale slowly. She does this sometimes, where she doesn't believe what one of us says until the other one independently confirms it. I think the police do it too. Me and Jamie have ended up very in sync because of this. If I ever get arrested, I hope it's with him.

"I will. I'm sorry."

Me and Jamie both leave the room awkwardly before high-fiving quietly in the hallway.

"Homework Club for the win," he whispers. Homework Club really is one of his best inventions. He's spent so long building it up that Mum's happy to believe every school has one. I'm not saying it's good to lie … but I am saying it's good to have a lie prepared in case you need it.

He ushers me into his room. "So where were you *actually*?" he asks.

Of course I haven't actually told him about the meeting with Ms George. I give him a quick rundown.

"So you just hung out, and she asked you questions about yourself?"

"Yeah, literally."

"But that's what friends would do."

"I know, it was so weird of her. But also kind of nice."

"*Wild*," he says. "Man, I kind of hate that we're at different schools. I feel like I don't really hang out with you any more."

"Yeah, there are a lot of drawbacks to segregation."

"Like, we used to see each other during every break, and we had all the same friends. Now everything's separate. It's like we're not even twins."

"That's probably because we aren't twins."

He shoves me slightly. "Jay, I'm sad."

Oh.

I suddenly realize that stuff with me and Jamie has been different since we moved here. I've been so busy between Mina and Alex that all we've talked about is that. He's right: we just used to know *everything* about each other, because we were always together. Before, we never really even had our own individual friends; we were always in the same groups together. I now feel so guilty for being distracted, because the more I think about it the more I realize how much I've missed having him around all the time.

"I'm sorry," I say. "I miss you too. How are things at the boys' school?"

"Oh, they're fine. I'm friends with everybody" – (of course he is) – "but I'm especially close with two guys. They're both called Tom."

"You're kidding."

"I'm not kidding. Tom Davidson, or Little Tom, and Tom Proctor, or Big Tom. Little Tom is really sweet and nerdy and Big Tom looks like a pro athlete who's pretending to be in high school. I call them the Toms."

"That makes sense."

"We all hung out last Friday. But I kept thinking it would have been more fun if you'd been there too."

I try to cheer him up the only way I know how: with gossip.

"Hey, guess what?"

"What?"

"Me and Mina have to go to a Planning Committee for the Summer Dance on Wednesday. Dani Hex leads it. She's stepping up her already strong insult game."

Jamie starts to perk up.

"Yeah? Did you finally find out what happened with her and Mina?"

"Both yes and no. Mina said they were best friends since they were little kids" – Jamie gasps – "but then a few months ago they had a fight at a party and haven't been friends since. But…" I pause for effect and Jamie's eyebrows raise in anticipation. "Mina says she doesn't remember what the fight was about."

"*No.*"

"Yes."

"But of course she does! Why would she keep this from us?"

"From me, I don't know. Maybe it's embarrassing? From you, she probably just hasn't assumed I'm going to tell you everything she says."

"That's fair enough. Don't worry, we'll get to the truth. Hey, what's the meanest thing Dani's said to you lately?"

"The other day she said it looked like I stole my shoes from a dead ballerina."

He whistles quietly. "Wow. That's so *specific*."

"I know. It's rare to receive an insult you've never heard before."

"It is. That's really cheered me up, thanks, Jay," he says.

"And I'm glad Ms George is so cool. Nice to have an adult you can actually talk to."

"I know. Maybe some people stay cool when they age. Now tell me more about the Toms! Do you have a favourite?"

We're right back to talking like we used to. I really do have the best brother. If there was some kind of Brother Olympics, with events like "being supportive" and "always cutting slices of cake the same size", he'd take home gold in everything.

CHAPTER 9

Tuesday, I oversleep and can't go skating and be distracted by Alex's good hair and mysterious angst.

Wednesday, he's there as I roll in. I'm tense, but you know what? Imaginary General Jamie was completely right. As far as Alex knows, nothing has changed. We quietly skate together like two totally normal skaters, one of whom is in disguise and obsessed with the other one. A tale as old as time. Everything is going to be fine.

When I walk through the school gates later that morning, Mina gives me a salute. "Feeling ready for the Planning Committee meeting?"

OK, not everything is going to be completely fine.

I glance nervously across the yard, to where Dani and her friends are staring fixedly at us and not speaking. "Well, *they* certainly are."

"Mm. They've been doing that for ten minutes already. I think I actually *love* the attention."

In form room Ms George gives a quick morning pep talk, and as me and Mina head back to the hallway, she whispers to us, "Good luck with the Planning Committee. I'm sure you're going to have a nice time."

It's kind of delightful that she thinks Dani is going to see the error of her ways and welcome us into the meeting with open arms. I wish I had that kind of faith that everything would work out for the best. I'd probably walk around befriending wild raccoons and juggling knives.

Dani spends the day reminding me and Mina that she does not like us.

DANI HEX'S TOP FIVE INSULTS (OF THE DAY)

1. (To me) "God, I don't know what it is, but I just can't remember your name. It must be that I don't care."
2. (To Mina) "Did you get shorter? Or wider?"
3. (To me) "Why is your hair like that? Did something happen?"

4. (To Mina) "I love your necklace!" (Again, this one's all in the delivery.)
5. (To both of us) "Well, if it isn't Heath Girls' cringiest couple."

That last one's actually kind of weak. As far as I know there aren't *any* couples in school, so technically speaking we'd also be the coolest. Still, every time she says something like that, I look at Mina nervously, like she's going to suddenly realize that Dani's only been making jokes about her going out with a girl since I showed up and no one would be questioning her sexuality if she didn't have me hanging around. But she acts like she hasn't heard it. Still, even though I'm sure Dani could make an A-list celebrity feel like an outsider if she wanted to, I feel like she's weirdly aware of some of the things I see in myself. Now that I'm dressed just like a girl and hanging out around a few hundred of them every day, I feel like if anything it's even clearer that I'm not quite like them – even the way I move and talk just seems slightly different. Maybe I'm imagining it, but it puts me on edge thinking Dani sees it too as she's the last person I want seeing into my soul. Actually, is that true? Who would be worse, Dani, Mum or Alex? God, I hope I never have to choose.

For the first time ever, the school day flies by. I guess that's what happens when you don't want it to. When the bell rings for the end of the day I feel a sinking sense of dread.

The thing is, I should be used to people like Dani Hex. Every teenager knows someone like her. Adults always make excuses for them – like "she feels small, or she wouldn't be treating other people the way she does". I don't know if that's true. I think Dani is having a great time, all the time. I think she likes being pretty. I think she likes being mean. She gets to do both, every day.

Me and Mina walk slowly towards the meeting room together.

"Mina, I don't wanna gooooo."

"Why? Are you not enjoying being bullied?"

I almost laugh. Dani Hex has nothing on my last bullies. "I wouldn't say I'm loving the experience, no."

"I'll be sure to pass that on to customer services. Listen up: game plan. I've written a flawless budget for them. They will argue with it, but Ms George will approve it, so whatever. I'll show it to them, remind them that it's not their decision and the more time they spend arguing with me the less time they can spend talking about dresses, and then me and you can just hang out in a corner until the meeting's over. Sound good?"

"Good might be pushing it, but it sounds OK."

"Great. Now remember…" She stops walking, grabs my shoulder and looks me in the eyes. Her eyes are so brown and warm when you're up close. Like teddy bears. Warm teddy bears. Teddy bears that are on fire? No, that's a terrible simile. Kind of upsetting actually.

Not for the first time, I hope she can't read minds. What was she saying? "We're cooler and hotter than all of them."

She turns away and walks into the room confidently.

I follow less confidently.

Dani and her friends are all sitting down. They've left two chairs free as far away as possible from the rest of them, which is probably meant to make us feel left out but is actually what I would have chosen.

"Mina," Dani says coldly, "and … is it Fay?" Oh, nice. Getting my name slightly wrong. She stares at me for long enough that I figure it's not a rhetorical question and I have to answer.

"Jay."

"*Jay*," she repeats, screwing up her nose. "Isn't that a boy's name?"

"Just a letter, really," I say, which makes Mina laugh. "Also, your name is Dani."

"So?"

"So Danny's a boy's name."

Her friends look at her for a response and her cheeks go slightly red.

"Can you read? It's spelled with an 'i'. So it's a girl's name."

"Sure, but you can't *hear* the 'i' when you say it out loud."

Dani scowls. "Can you stop delaying my meeting?"

I can't help but smirk slightly, and Mina looks like she's trying not to crack up. I totally won that round.

We sit down.

"OK, so first of all—" Dani starts, but Mina cuts her off, sliding copies of her budget along the table for everyone to take.

"Here's your budget," she says.

Irritated, Dani snatches one up. "Well, this is nowhere *near* enough money."

"That's all the money we get, Dani. I've written out how you should spend it."

"Well…" Dani scans the budget, looking for something wrong. "Well … well, it's…"

"It's perfect and Ms George is going to approve it, so why don't we move on?" Mina says with a sweet smile. Dani glares at her, but she's obviously lost. Again. Me and Mina are kind of nailing it today.

"*Fine*," Dani says. "At least we don't have to do the nerd work."

"Thanks, Mina!" says one of Dani's friends, before Dani glares her into silence.

"Let's officially begin the meeting," Dani says, trying to take control again. "The hard work comes later, but this term's meeting is the most exciting part: picking the theme!"

"How about something ocean-themed?" another girl chips in. (I've really got to learn their names. Or at least make some up.)

"Under the Sea was literally the theme in 2018," Dani snaps.

Millicent looks sad. (I don't know, it's the first name that came to mind.)

"Sure, but you could do something like *Baywatch*, right? Lifeguards, surfers, flower necklaces..." Mina says.

"Oh, that's a great idea!" says Janice. (I don't know where I'm getting these names from.)

I wasn't expecting to watch a power struggle unfold, but I have to say I'm enjoying it. Everyone seems to like Mina's idea, which makes Dani furious. It's fun seeing someone so enraged over just the concept of a flower necklace.

I so badly want to know what their fight was about.

"Do you think the teachers would let people wear just, like, bikinis and swim shorts?" Janice continues excitedly. "I bet Alex has a six pack. Have you seen his arms?"

"There is no *way*," Dani snaps, shutting off her cooing friends, "they'll allow it. Even taking photos at a dance like that would be illegal."

Everyone looks disappointed, except me and Mina, who are shaking with silent laughter, watching Dani get angrier and angrier.

"Besides, only *I* get to see Alex's six pack," Dani says.

My heart plummets. God, there are just so many reasons that I hate her.

"Are you guys dating?" Hannah asks. (That's actually her name; she's in Ms George's form too.)

"Let's talk about it later," Dani says, glancing at me and Mina.

"So you're not dating?" Mina says.

"I haven't seen him much because there haven't been any good parties lately," Dani says breezily, like she's a Manhattan socialite who attends balls every weekend, not a fourteen-year-old in a small town. "Not that you'd know, because you'd never be invited."

"Oh my god!" says Janice. "I should have a New Year's Eve party! My parents are away, and we can invite everyone. It'd be the perfect chance for you to finally hook up with Alex!"

"We've, like, basically hooked up loads of times," Dani says, but at this point even I can tell it's not true. I can't help smiling. I mean, I know Alex probably likes girls that look like Dani (because she's pretty), but I'm glad he doesn't like her specifically (because she's a monster).

They all throw out theme suggestions for a while: Brides and Grooms, which Dani points out would look like a mass wedding in quite a creepy way; Doctors and Nurses, which Dani thinks won't give the girls enough dress options; Beauty and the Beast, which Dani decides the boys will ruin by dressing like monsters; Mermaids and Cowboys, a rogue suggestion from Janice (who I'm really starting to like) that everybody agrees is too out there. How would a mermaid and a cowboy even meet? Cowboys are famously land-based. The list goes on, and

Dani isn't pleased with any of them – until she pulls out her trump card.

"I actually think I have a really good idea," she says modestly, pulling a file out of her bag. *Of course* she waited to undermine everybody else first. "Ladies," she says, "what do we think … about a Pink and Blue dance?"

She swings open the folder to reveal what I have to admit is a well-put-together mood board. Dresses ranging from blush to hot pink, suits from powder to midnight blue. Girls with elaborate pink eye make-up. She's used paint swatches to decorate the background, and stuck example decorations around the borders.

"Oh my god, it's so cute!" her friends gasp.

"Right?" she says. "Think how good it'll look in the photos!"

Mina rolls her eyes at me, but I think she'd look really nice in a blush pink dress. She does that thing sometimes where she matches her eyeshadow to something in her outfit, and that would look really cool. And not to toot my own horn, but blue has always been a good colour on me. I could wear a midnight blue suit with a really light blue shirt, with no tie; I always think that looks cool, suits with no ties. I look at Dani's mocked-up photo backdrop with pink and blue paint splashed across it, and imagine how cool me and Mina would look in front of it.

"It's so easy," Dani goes on. "Girls in pink dresses, boys

in blue suits. Everyone knows exactly what to wear, so no one will mess up the theme."

Oh.

Yeah. Of course. I wasn't thinking.

Girls in pink, boys in blue. A different image cuts into my head of me in a hideous, frilly, hot pink dress, looking like a depressed, androgynous shrimp. I feel sick imagining pulling it on. I can almost hear how Mum would tell me how lovely I look while I stare at the dress, appalled. Wearing a dull, grey uniform skirt is one thing, but being expected to get all glittered up and try to look pretty makes me feel like I'm trapped in a horror movie.

I stand frozen in a dark hallway, breathing heavily. Violin music builds to a crescendo as I shake with fear. Suddenly a curtain at the end of the hall swings open, revealing a grotesque lady holding lipsticks and brushes. She starts lurching towards me, yelling something about contouring, and I start to scream as the walls begin to bleed (I'm not sure why the walls are bleeding but it suits the mood...)

Obviously no one else in the room is experiencing this vivid waking nightmare in response to the Pink and Blue theme, so it's settled.

"Well," Mina says, as we finally leave Dani and her friends behind, "at least they didn't go with Brides and Grooms. Can you imagine? All the girls in white gowns? Unsettling."

"I'm kind of sad Mermaids and Cowboys didn't go anywhere. I loved that. It didn't make any sense at all."

"Ah, yes, Elena's contribution. She's always been a little spacey."

"Oh, her name's Elena? I thought it was Janice."

Mina laughs. "Why?"

"She kind of looks like a Janice."

"I know what you mean. Anyway, how do you feel about the theme? No offence, but I can't really imagine you wearing pink."

"Yeah, pink isn't really my thing. I think I look better in blue."

"I can see that," Mina says quietly.

I don't know if she understands what I mean or if she's just being nice. But either way, it feels good to hear her agree.

"Anyway," she says, "see you tomorrow. I expect you to bring a selection of gowns for me to try on. Don't forget the accessories: I'm thinking elbow-length gloves."

She waves and heads down the street in the opposite direction from me. I walk home slowly, wondering what Mina would say if she saw me wearing clothes that I liked.

Jamie is waiting in the hall when I walk into the house.

"OK, quick: what was the meanest thing Dani said to you in the meeting?"

"She said Jay was a boy's name, and I pointed out that 'Danny' is also a boy's name. She was furious. It felt good."

He laughs. "Well done. I didn't think you had it in you."

"Me neither. Oh, and don't tell your friends because they haven't announced it yet, but the theme for this year's Summer Dance is Pink and Blue."

"What, like babies? Like boys in blue and girls in pink?"

"Yup. Blue suits and pink dresses. Which is fine. I guess."

You know what? Jamie is too intuitive. He's giving me that sympathetic look that shows he knows exactly what I'm feeling, and for SOME REASON that immediately makes me start to cry. I can't remember the last time I cried properly. This has come on so fast.

Jamie hustles me into his room so we don't have to try to explain this to Mum. "Oh, Jay," he says. "I'm so sorry. Don't cry, it's OK."

"I don't want to wear a dress," I sob out. "I don't want to wear this skirt."

"I know," he says. "I know."

"I look so bad, Jamie," I continue, ugly crying. "I hate how I look right now. I hate my hair." I slump down on the edge of his bed, head in my hands. "I hate it, and I hate Mum."

That feels horrible to say out loud, but it's a bit true. I'm so angry. The only thing that makes me feel better is knowing I have my skateboard and that I can go to the skatepark in the morning without her knowing. I can't handle the idea of her finding out, but for some reason it makes me feel a kind of cold happiness knowing how shocked she'd be if she did. Jamie keeps patting me on the back until the sobs turn into hiccups.

"Sorry," I say.

"Don't be. Maybe we should talk to Mum? Maybe you could persuade her to let you wear trousers at school. Then you'd feel a bit better about things?"

I wipe my cheeks. "I don't know if I can even try. She's different with you; you never *disappoint* her like I do. When I wear The Skirt, she doesn't seem disappointed any more."

I think this might be the first time I've seen Jamie truly lost for words. He's trying desperately to think of something helpful.

"Want to play that game where we pretend we're gonna slap each other's hands and if anyone flinches then you actually get to slap their hands?"

I smile. He always knows just what to say. "Yes."

CHAPTER 10

Somehow, it's almost half-term already. Despite the lowlight of Dani and the Planning Committee, there's been the highlights of meeting Mina and Alex to balance things out, and I'm actually pretty proud of myself for making it so long without reducing Mum to tears. Or revealing my secret identity.

On the last day before half-term, Alex is at the skatepark before me. I give him a wave as I roll in. As I start practising hardflips, I can't stop thinking about what Dani said about him at the meeting. She likes him. I wonder whether he likes her back. He must. She's, like, the perfect girl. Well, you'd think so, anyway, if she kept her demon side hidden.

Obviously I can't just ask him about it; you can't just out-of-the-blue ask a guy you barely speak to if he likes a girl he would have no reason to believe you've ever met — you know, being homeschooled and all. I go back to practising hardflips in silence.

But curiosity gets the better of me almost immediately.

"So do you hang out with anyone from the girls' school?" I ask. "Because you said how you don't really like the guys from your school. So I thought maybe you would like the girls. From another school." Please make me stop talking.

He shrugs. "Like, a girlfriend? Honestly, I just go to school, read and skate. Is that boring?"

"Not at all. It's kind of cool, actually."

"Why?"

"You do what you want."

"Thanks." He looks quite pleased.

I'm pretty pleased that he hasn't even mentioned Dani. Maybe he doesn't even know who she is.

"What about you?" he asks. "Do you have a girlfriend, or whatever?"

"No, I'm like you," I say.

He stares at me. "What do you mean?"

"I mean, I do my homework and I skate. I don't really have time for anything else."

"Sure," he says, and we lapse into our usual skateboarding silence. I don't know if I'm imagining it, but I feel like we look at each other a lot. Does that mean something? I'm acting like we're a man and a woman at some sort of ball in the eighteenth century or something.

"Lady Mina, do not look now, but Lord Alexander glances this way yet again!"

"My goodness," says the Lady Mina. "This speaks of some special affection, does it not?"

I blush delicately and smooth my petticoats.

"I wouldn't dare guess at the intentions of his heart. Though I must admit, I am well pleased."

"You are too timid!" exclaims the Lady Mina, clasping both of my hands in hers and gazing into my eyes. "He pays you uncommon attention; his looks surely speak of deeper desire. I shouldn't be surprised to hear of an engagement within the fortnight…"

GOD it's a large crush. I like that he feels as though he doesn't fit in too. In fact, apart from Jamie, he's the only person in my life right now who knows me as I am. Even if he doesn't know much about me, and most of what he does know isn't strictly true, and he probably thinks I'm a guy … he sees Jay, not Jennifer. Not that he likes me the same way I like him – I know *that*.

I still remember what Mum said to me as we drove out of London: "Who's going to be attracted to you if you keep dressing like that?"

It hurt, but it's true. Nobody's ever had a crush on me.

Nobody's ever really told me I look good, except Jamie, and you'll be thrilled to hear there's no crush there. But friends like Alex and Mina, that can be enough.

Anything else is just asking to get hurt.

WINTER

WINTER

CHAPTER 11

Now, I don't really like school. It's boring. There are weird rules. Historically, I haven't been the most popular. But even *I* like school around Christmastime. I don't know what it is, but the second they put streamers and paper chains up in the hallway I get warm fuzzy feelings. It kind of reminds me of primary school, when things were simpler. People didn't seem to care about my hair or clothes then, they just wanted to know when I was done with the glitter so they could use it. The nostalgia makes it a bit better when it's so cold and dark all the time. Even Alex, a committed T-shirt wearer, has started wearing a jumper.

"What's up, Jay!" he calls as I roll into the skatepark,

which is just barely bright enough to see from the street lamps on the road.

"Today's the day, Alex," I say dramatically. "I'm going to land a 5-0 on the rail. I can feel it."

"Sick," he says.

I've been trying to land a 5-0 for weeks now. It's when you grind along something while balancing on the back truck of your board (the metal bit that holds the wheels on). I *know* I can do it, I've done them on kerbs and ledges before, but I'm always a little skittish when it comes to rails. I mean, why wouldn't you be? They're made of metal. Have you ever fallen on metal? It's not fun.

Alex takes out his phone. "Here, I'll film you."

"I'll try not to let the fame go to my head," I say.

He smiles.

We've known each other for a few months now, and I think I can call us friends at this point. I feel like I kind of know him. Like, he never makes jokes, but he really likes it when I do. His whole face lights up, even though he never says anything back. I think he's too shy to try to be funny. In fact, I think he's pretty shy in general – that's why he doesn't talk very much, and has all those long brooding silences. It feels like he has secrets too. I bet they're cool secrets, like he's a vampire, or he's been to prison or something. No, those aren't cool, why have teen movies warped my mind? The more I get to know him, the more I want to know him.

Yes, I still have a crush on him. And yes, it's getting worse.

It takes me four tries, but I finally decide that if I fall on to a metal rail today that's just my destiny, and land a sketchy 5-0. We both mess around, whooping and throwing our skateboards in celebration.

"I got it on camera!" he says. "Let me get your number; I'll send it to you."

"Awesome," I say, heading over to type it into his phone. I expect him to send it to me straight away, but instead he slips his phone back into his pocket, which sends me instantly into a tailspin. Does this mean he's going to text me later instead? If he does, are we going to have a conversation? Can I handle that?

Of course I can handle that. We just had a live conversation with our mouths. If anything, having one in writing should be easier.

"What are you thinking about?" Alex asks suddenly.

I wonder if I'll ever be having a thought that's not too weird to share when someone asks me that.

"The Christmas holidays," I say, trying to think of something, "and, like, New Year's Eve and stuff. Pretty close now."

"Ah," he says, nodding. "Are you allowed to celebrate that?"

We still haven't gone into the details of which religion I'm pretending to be.

"Sure," I say.

"Do you have plans for New Year's Eve?"

"Nah," I say, "it's hard to get to know anybody in town with being homeschooled. I might do something with my friends from, uh … church. What about you?"

"I'm going to a party." He sighs.

"Well, don't act too excited about it, Alex."

He grins. "I don't really want to go. But, like, it feels worse not to do anything at all and just stay home."

"What's the party?"

"This girl from the girls' school is having a big one," he says.

Knew it. That has to be Elena's party. I think me and Mina are actually becoming friends with Elena. She's so excited about the party; I've had a few conversations with her about how she's planning to decorate and stuff (she suggested eggs, to represent "new beginnings", and I told her that was not exactly tradition and a little bit odd, and she took it in her stride). She's actually really nice, and she's even said a few times that me and Mina should come – but we all know that's not up to her. It's up to Dani.

"Why don't you come with me?" he says abruptly.

I freeze. This is the first time there's been a risk of Jay and Jennifer being in the same room. For a hot second, I think, *why not?* Just show up dressed as a boy. Who's gonna notice? Then I tell myself I'm losing it – *everyone would notice.* But lately I'm getting this weird feeling, like …

I *want* to take risks. Maybe I want someone to catch me, even. Last night Mum said my hair looked nice now that it's longer, and I felt this huge urge to walk straight to the bathroom and cut it all off. I even stood up, but I caught myself. I still want Mum to be happy, I do.

But keeping her that way might make me explode. Like a bomb. That's also tired of trying to keep its mother happy.

And THEN I think a) I might be happier if I didn't think so much and b) did Alex just … ask me out?? Obviously not in a date way, but still. Why would Alex invite me to a party with him?

"Really? But I wouldn't know anybody."

"You'd know me. You'd be with me."

We smile at each other for a second. It's like this with Alex sometimes. Something about the way we talk to each other feels a little … strange. It's hard to describe. I guess what I mean is that I've had guy friends before, and those friendships haven't been like this. He's offering to take me to a party and hang out with me all night so I won't be anxious. It's sweet and protective.

Or am I reading too much into this? Again?

"That's true…" I say.

"I know your mum is strict," he says, "but let me talk to the girl having the party and see if I can have a plus one. Just in case."

I know there's no way I can go with Alex. But I *really*

want to. And what's the harm in playing along for now? To be polite?

"OK. That would be cool."

It's sunrise by the time I sneak back into my room. I put on my sad little skirt and look in the mirror. My hair's shoulder length now. I find myself hiding behind it. It's getting harder to tie up and hide under the cap when I go skating.

I hate this. I hate what I see in the mirror. Something has to give.

"I don't know if I can take it any more, Jamie," I say, on the walk to school.

"The crumbling state of the world? The pressures of secondary school?"

"Well, sure. But really – the hair. The Skirt."

"Yeah." He sighs.

"I feel like I'm going to snap," I tell him. Like I'm going to do something reckless."

"I hear that, and I would love to see it," he says, "but you should probably … not. For both our sakes. There must be a reckful way to handle this." He sighs again. "But you don't look right."

"I don't feel right, either. You're the mastermind, Jamie. What do we do?"

"Maybe you could tell Mum you're going to wear trousers? Start there?" he says, half-heartedly.

"You know exactly what would happen. Full Sad Mum."

128

It feels a little tense when I say this, and I know it's because we disagree. He doesn't understand why I won't just give up and do what I want, like I used to. Of course he doesn't get it. She's always been proud of him. It's like if Santa had asked Rudolph to guide the sleigh and one of the other reindeer (let's say Dasher) had been like, "Don't do that, man, he's only come to you because he needs something." Dasher doesn't have anything to prove. Rudolph does. Even if it makes him feel bad about himself. Look, I'm not sure if this seasonal metaphor is standing up, but it's how I feel.

"All right," he says. "Well, you and Mina are close, right?"

"The term 'best friends' has been thrown around," I say proudly. My friendship with Mina is something that feels really, really … good. I want to show off about it.

"Why don't you tell *her* what you're really like? Get another person in your corner."

"Out of the question. She knows enough."

"She knows your name is Jay and that you don't want to wear a pink ballgown. That's barely half of the truth," he says. "Mina's one of the coolest people I've ever met. Do you really think she's gonna ditch you if she finds out you want a buzzcut?"

"I don't want to find out. And I *don't* want a buzzcut; you *know* I like it longer on the top."

He subconsciously pushes a hand through his own hair,

ruffling up the top. He's looking taller and broader around the shoulders, filling out his school shirts more. I feel a pang of jealousy.

"You know what I mean. Why are you so scared of telling her?"

"It would just … change things. It would change the dynamic. I don't know. She made friends with a girl."

"Jay, she made friends with you."

"Well. Sort of."

"If you won't tell her, why don't you tell Alex?"

"Oh yeah, that'll go well. Tell him that I've been lying to him all these months?"

"You've never told him you're a guy."

"No. But I have told him that I'm homeschooled by an incredibly strict and generically religious mother."

"Still haven't said which religion, huh?"

"Nope. And again, I'm not telling him. He made friends with that guy."

"And again – he made friends with *you*."

Jamie's sweet, but he's wrong. Nobody in Hatch Heath knows me. They know a fake version of me. Jamie throws his hands up in despair.

"Try to tell someone *something* real about yourself, Jay," he says. "I think it might be good for you."

Yeah, right. Not all of us have the luxury of knowing people will like the real us. Wow, that was angsty.

"Jay!" Mina says happily when I walk into our classroom. "Can you believe you've nearly finished your first term as a Heath Girl?"

"I can't believe it at all. What's my reward?"

"Another term," she says cheerfully.

"Oh, great."

"You're welcome. Want to do something after school?"

"I've got my meeting with Ms George," I remind her. I'm still meeting her, and I'm still meeting Hugo – and no, I don't like Hugo any better. Turns out first impressions can be correct. Our sessions now consist of me sitting in silence while he tries to get a rise out of me by recounting the worst events of my life. I don't know why he thinks it's going to work. I was there. I already know what happened.

"Ah, yes. Ms George, your other best friend. I'll try not to get too jealous."

I laugh, but it actually feels almost true. I have a great time in Ms George's sessions, and I think she does too. Unless she's a great actor. They're, like, the opposite of the sessions with Hugo because she doesn't try to make me talk about anything in particular. We just talk about TV shows, or the Wars of the Roses (not because that's what we're into; I'm studying it in history). It feels nice, just being able to talk about little stuff without thinking too much.

School has that end-of-term feeling, like people have already mentally checked out of classes. The only thing anybody's talking about is Elena's party. It's shaping up to be the highlight of the year's social calendar (apart from the Summer Dance, of course). It seems like everyone's going from both schools – Jamie doesn't even know her and *he's* been invited along with his friends. Elena seems remarkably calm for someone who is almost undoubtedly about to have their house completely destroyed. Maybe she doesn't realize. Dani's always saying she's "not exactly smart", but that's not true. She's just a little … surreal. We sit next to each other in biology and she comes out with a lot of weird questions like "Can the sea think?" When I pressed her on that one, she explained that every metre of the sea is full of microbes and stuff, which are kind of like the cells in our brains. She had me stumped. Maybe the sea *does* think. See what I mean? Actually pretty smart.

When we walk into biology, she gestures me and Mina over.

"Hey, guys," she whispers.

"Why are we whispering?" I whisper.

"You know my party?"

"The whole school knows about your party, yes," Mina whispers.

"Well, I want you to come."

"Are you whispering because you don't want Dani to know that?"

"Yes."

"Dani's not in this class."

"That's true," she says, continuing to whisper. Maybe she thinks Dani can hear through walls. "I just think it's unfair that I'm not allowed to be friends with you because you and her had a fight," she says to Mina.

"Did she tell you what the fight was about?" Mina sounds nervous.

"No. She won't talk about it. The point is, I want you to come to the party. And, Jay, you've been so nice helping me decide on decorations. You were right, eggs would have been weird. So I want you to come too."

"Thanks, Elena," I say. "Can we stop whispering?"

"No," she whispers. "I'm terrified of Dani."

"We all should be if she can hear us from a totally different classroom."

"She doesn't have to hear us *herself*."

See? Pretty smart, this one.

"You're not going to tell her that we're coming, are you?" Mina whispers.

"Absolutely not. I'm going to act surprised and kind of annoyed. But *you'll* know that I'm pleased."

"I love the sentiment, Elena, but I don't think that's the best idea," Mina murmurs thoughtfully. "She might get us physically thrown out if she thinks we're crashing. Why don't you just say that your parents insisted you invite the whole class?"

Elena looks at Mina, impressed. "That's a great idea."

Mina bows.

After class I lean over to her. "Did we just add another friend to our group?"

"Two people isn't really a group, is it?"

"But three are!"

"I think we have! But a secret friend. It's kind of like we're having an affair."

Dani sits at the kitchen table, staring sadly at the clock. Elena said she was working late at the office. Again. Does she really expect her to believe that? If it wasn't for the kids, Dani would walk out right now...

"It *is* kind of like that, yeah."

We walk to the canteen to grab sandwiches. I buy a flapjack for us to share, and Mina manages to hack off a slice of her apple for me with a butter knife. We sit together at our usual lunch table, slightly apart from the rest of the school. I love having lunch with her like this. If I was going to tell Mina something personal, this would be the time and place to do it. No one would overhear us.

"You know," she says suddenly, "I want to see you skating!"

Wow, where did that come from?

"Uh ... maybe sometime if my mum goes out of town."

"Jay," she says carefully, "what's the deal with your mum?"

I blink. This really would be the perfect time to open up. But my tone is cold when I speak. "Just like I told you,"

I say, "she doesn't like stuff she doesn't think is feminine, or whatever."

"Mmmm. That seems kind of weird, though. That she would stop you from skating, and – correct me if I'm wrong – refuse to call you Jay even though that's what you like being called."

"She's not *stopping* me from skating."

"Sweetie," she says, teasingly, "you are not as good a liar as you think you are."

I slowly chew my mouthful of apple, and we're silent.

Then, halfway through the apple, I realize: I want to tell Mina the truth. I want her to know what I really look like. I even maybe want to tell her what happened at my last school, and even laugh about it with her, because it's over now. I think she'd feel sorry for me, but I don't think she'd *pity* me. I want to tell her all of it.

But what I say is: "I don't want to talk about it."

She sets her jaw. "All right. Fine."

It's awkward for the rest of the day.

"Someone looks grumpy," Ms George says when I arrive for our after-school session.

"Someone *is*," I say.

"Well, come on. Why?"

I don't want to tell her anything. She's an adult. What does she know? How could she possibly understand? I'm not going to tell her anything.

What happens is:

I start crying.

"I had a fight with Mina because she asked to see me skateboarding and I said I can't because of my mum so she asked why and I didn't want to tell her but I do want to tell her and I want to tell her everything about my last school too but I didn't."

I've caught us both by surprise. For several seconds we just look at each other and blink.

"I have never seen you display this much emotion," she says.

Despite the crying, I laugh a bit.

"Why don't we start at the beginning, Jay? Do you think we could do that? As I'm sure you've guessed, I know more about you and your last school than you've told me – but I'd like to hear it all from you."

I take a deep breath. "Can I use your phone to show you something?"

"Sure – is yours out of battery?"

"No, my mum just won't let me have one with internet."

She raises her eyebrows but hands me her phone, and I navigate to my old school's website. I flick through to the page about extracurricular activities – you know, the page where a school is like, "*Look how awesome we are, we can teach your kids to play the clarinet*" or whatever.

There's a picture there of me and Jamie. I remember the day. When the photographer took it, he handed us a basketball and said, "Pretend to play." It was awkward, but the picture came out really well. Jamie's trying to block me from making a shot and we're both laughing. I hand the phone back for her to look at the photo.

"Who am I looking at?" she asks.

"That's me and my brother."

She gasps and looks closer.

Actual me. Me and Jamie are wearing identical uniforms: white button-up shirts and black trousers. He's wearing a tie; I'm not, but you can see it slightly hanging out of my trouser pocket. I have one of my favourite hairstyles: the back of my hair is cut close to my scalp, but the front is flopping forward over my eyes. I felt like me. I want to look like that again so much that I feel sick. I miss that whole time, when Mum would roll her eyes and say "I do wish you'd wear a dress once in a while, Jay", but not get upset about it. Before those girls in my class started being mean, and Mum's anxiety about me started getting worse and worse.

"I read the notes in your file about what happened at your last school," she says quietly. "Is the way you dressed back then part of the reason why?"

I nod. "Do *you* think it was my fault?"

She looks shocked. "Of *course* not. Do *you* think that?"

I shrug. "I chose to dress that way even though Mum always warned me some people wouldn't like it."

"That's their problem, not yours."

"Well. I ended up getting hurt, and Mum was so scared it would happen again…"

"So it's your mother who wants you to wear that skirt. And your hair…" Maybe this is my ego talking, but I think she looks sad as she glances between the photo and me. Like she knows how cool my hair *could* look.

"I hate my hair," I say, tugging at it.

"Jay, did your mother force you to grow your hair?"

"No, it's not like that. She just wants me to be someone … more like her, I guess. She wanted to move so we could have a fresh start. She suggested I grow my hair to fit in. Then she suggested the skirt. And when I said I'd try, it seemed like she was … *proud* of me instead of worried about me for the first time."

"What happened must have really scared her."

"I'd rather not talk about it," I say.

"OK. Listen, Jay: why don't I have a chat with your mother? I might be able to reassure her. This is an open-minded and accepting school."

Is it really that easy? Could I really just ask Ms George to talk to Mum and then I can go back to dressing how I want to?

Then I flashback to the days after the accident, when Mum wouldn't stop crying so hard it was like she couldn't breathe…

Of course things can't be that easy.

"This school has a zero tolerance policy to bullying, particularly homophobic bullying," Ms George continues.

"Yeah, my last school said that too. Though I'm actually

not gay," I say cheerfully. I'm not going to tell her about my crush (god, imagine), but I am quite excited to tell somebody that I'm not as gay as everyone thinks.

"Oh. I'm sorry for assuming."

"No, no, it would make sense. I might be, a bit. Who knows, really?"

"There's no need to rush to figure that out."

"Thanks."

It's actually kind of nice to hear somebody say that. I continue, "But however open-minded you think this school is, there's no girl here who looks like *that*." I point at the picture on her phone.

"Not now, but there have been in the past! And there's nothing wrong with being unique."

"It hasn't worked out so well for me, historically."

"You didn't have *me* then. Or Mina," she says. "I can promise you right now that I won't let anything like that happen to you here. I mean it."

I look at her. Her expression is very earnest. She straightens her brightly patterned shawl around her shoulders like she's preparing for battle. I know people don't usually wear shawls to battle, but she's managing to make it look very military and serious.

"Can anyone really stop that sort of thing happening?"

"They can try," she says firmly.

I mean, sure, I'd prefer a one hundred per cent guarantee, but that might be the nicest thing an adult – and certainly a teacher — has ever said to me. No one really tried to stop things at my last school. They acted like I was the problem.

"Thank you."

"Why don't you wear trousers tomorrow? Start small."

"She only bought me skirts for school, and … I don't want to make her sad again."

"OK," Ms George says gently.

I glance at the clock. We've run a little over time.

"I should go," I say. "Don't want to get home too late."

"All right," she says. "But when you are ready to make some changes, just know that I'll be there. OK?"

I actually believe that she will.

"Thanks."

When I get home, I find Mum and Jamie in the living room. Jamie is on the floor half-heartedly doing some homework while Mum sits on the couch wholeheartedly doing a crossword. Adults love those, they must be like video games to them. We make small talk until Mum goes to start cooking and Jamie and I settle into an actual conversation.

"So, did you manage to tell someone something about yourself today?"

"You know what? I did."

"And how do you feel?"

"You were right. I feel good."

"Called it! So, was it Mina?"

"Nope."

"Alex, then?"

"Nope."

"Not your new friend Elena? That's rogue."

"Ms George."

"An *adult*?"

"I know. I didn't mean to do it, it just happened."

"Well, regardless, I'm proud of you."

I'm kind of proud of me too.

CHAPTER 12

The next morning I skate with Alex and change the subject every time he brings up Elena's party. I know I have to say no soon, but it's nice to stretch out the fantasy that I could go with him in the clothes I like, and we could hang out talking in a corner because he'd rather be with me than anyone else and then he could propose to me at midnight. You know?

At school, things are still a little weird with Mina. She's friendly, and I'm friendly, but it feels like we're being awkwardly formal with each other. I want to try to fix it, but I don't know how.

"So," I say, as we sit silently at lunch. It's the last day

of term. We should be happy. "Are we going to Elena's party?"

"Definitely."

"Together?"

"Obviously."

"I mean you do sound absolutely *furious* with me."

"I *am*. But I'm not going to a party alone."

Even though she's angry, we're both giggling now.

"Look, I'm sorry, I should know, but why are you annoyed at me?"

"Because you don't tell me anything. You haven't told me a single thing about your last school, or what's going on with your mum. We're supposed to be friends, but you're keeping stuff from me. I don't get it."

I'm annoyed, and she sees it immediately on my face.

"Why are *you* annoyed now?"

"Well, you keep things from me too, Mina."

"What?! I do not."

"Oh, yeah? Why did you and Dani really fall out, then?"

The look of shock on her face tells me two things. One: there *is* more to the Dani story than she's letting on. And two: she really did not think I was observant.

"Ha! I knew I was right."

"W-well … the – the thing is…" She stammers a bit and then stops. It's weird seeing Mina on the back foot.

"It's OK," I tell her. "We don't need to tell each other everything."

"There's a difference between not telling someone *everything* and not telling someone *anything*, Jay." She grabs her tray and stands up abruptly.

"Whoa, what? Are you storming off?"

"Yes, I am! Don't follow me! *Let me storm!*"

She storms. I'm left sitting at the table alone, stunned.

I wipe the champagne Mina just threw at me from my eyes and try to maintain my composure as she storms out of the fancy restaurant we're in. The waiter appears quietly at my side with a napkin.

"Sir … I will have to ask that you leave," he says discreetly.

"I understand," I reply, throwing a handful of crumpled notes on to the table and running out of the restaurant on to the dark, rain-soaked street, looking desperately for Mina. I don't know where she went, but I know I have to follow her…

Really, I'm still just sitting alone in a canteen. At least I don't have to chase her through 1920s New York, like in my fantasy. We sit next to each other in history.

As Ms George talks about the War of the Roses (we're learning about Richard Neville. Did you know they called him the Kingmaker? Why aren't nicknames that cool any more?), I slip Mina a note: SORRY.

She gives me a half smile and nods, and I know it's OK. We walk out of the gates together at the end of the day.

"All right, so obviously I won't see you over the next few days, with Christmas and everything," she says, "but let's hang out in between Christmas and Elena's party?"

"I'd really like that."

"Great. We'll go out for cocktails."

"Perfect. I'll find a long trench coat so you can sit on my shoulders and we'll look like one long adult."

"Cute. Thanks for letting me be the face."

"In this duo you're the beauty, I'm the legs."

"Don't you mean the brains?"

"No."

She laughs. "Great. I warn you, I have an ulterior motive. I'm hoping you let something slip about your mysterious past once you're a few cocktails in."

"I won't be talking at all, Mina. Legs don't talk."

She pulls me into a hug while poking me in the ribs at the same time to remind me that she's still a little bit annoyed at me. I hug her back while trying to block her jabs.

"Have a good Christmas, Legs. I'll see you soon."

"Have a good Christmas, Beauty," I say back, as Jamie comes over.

He raises his eyebrows, and I immediately realize how that sounded and turn bright red.

"See ya, Jamie," she calls back, heading to her dad's car.

"See ya, Mina!" He turns to me. "Sorry for *interrupting*."

"What do you mean?"

"Well, you know. You were having a little cuddle."

"We were not."

"You were. That's literally what you were doing."

"We were having a Christmas hug."

"Is that what the kids call it these days?"

"Shut up."

"Is she going to be at Elena's? I really want to hang out with her properly."

"Yeah, she is. Just don't embarrass me in front of her."

He giggles. "Sorry. I'll rein it in. I don't want to upset your Beauty."

I start chasing him, trying to smack him with my backpack. "We were doing a bit! That nickname made a lot of sense in context!"

"Is the context that you're in love with her?"

I chase him all the way back. When we walk in the door, we stop laughing immediately.

Something is wrong.

There's a tense silence in the house. Like when you go outside just before a thunderstorm and the sky's the wrong colour and you can feel the electricity.

Jamie looks at me with a mix of anxiety and concern. It's never him who's in trouble.

"Jennifer," Mum's voice comes from the living room, "would you come in here, please?"

Jamie follows me down the hallway and takes up a position outside the living-room door where he can listen.

"Hi, Mum," I say as I walk in. She's sitting very still in the exact centre of the couch. She's clearly been stress tidying the room. Things are too neat. Tears are already shimmering in her eyes. What have I done this time? *Please tell me she didn't find the skateboard.*

"Do you know how much your brother and I gave up so that you could have a fresh start?"

I do know the answer to that. "Yes."

"And you're choosing to throw it all away?"

I stay quiet.

"Did you not think I'd get an end of term report?"

Oh no. Ms George. I can just imagine how it all went. Her thinking she was doing me a favour, that everything would be better if she just spoke to my mother for me... I told her not to. I *told* her.

"So you've just been sitting there in silence, refusing to talk to Hugo? Not even *trying*?"

Hugo!

"He says your friends call you *Jay*."

Mum's hands are shaking and she's starting to cry. It's time to start talking. All I want is to stop the spiral before it starts.

First tactic: deny responsibility.

"It's not my fault, Mum," I say. "Mina started using it as a nickname, just shortening my name. You know, J. It caught on."

She narrows her eyes. "And why aren't you talking to Hugo?"

"It's ... hard," I say, scrambling for some emotion. If she

147

thinks I'm upset, maybe she'll feel bad for me. "What happened is so hard to talk about. I'm trying."

"You said that you *wanted* to change and try to fit in," she says, her voice shaking. "Was that a lie?"

For a little while, I really felt like it wasn't. I felt so horrible at the time I would have tried anything to feel better. But now that I'm in the lie, I don't know how to get out of it without upsetting Mum like this.

"Of course not," I say woodenly. "It is what I want."

"I just want you to be happy and safe," she says. "That's why we left our lives behind for you."

"I didn't ask you to do that," I point out. I regret it as I say it.

The explosion happens. Mum is sobbing on the couch, inconsolable. She always says the same kind of things through the tears. "I'm a terrible mother"; "I can't do anything right"; "it's all my fault". I try to comfort her. Jamie comes in and tries too. But there's nothing we can do.

"I thought you finally wanted to act like a daughter!"

Me and Jamie both freeze. I don't think she realizes how painful her words are, but they stop both of us in our tracks.

"Just leave me alone," she weeps, and, in the end, we do.

We go into Jamie's room and sit on the bed, shell-shocked. We can still hear the sobbing.

"Do you think this is a bad time to ask if I can go stay at Mina's on the twenty-ninth?" I whisper.

He snorts and claps a hand over his face to muffle it.

We both start giggling uncontrollably, stuffing our faces into pillows. I know we both feel bad for laughing, but every time this happens we just have so much nervous energy. It has to go somewhere.

A few hours later, Jamie and I slink over to the kitchen table for what I suspect will not be an easy dinner.

Mum places plates of salmon, potatoes and green beans in front of us without saying a word. She sits down. Our knives and forks scrape as we start to eat. Everyone stares at their food.

I crack.

"I'll talk to Hugo," I say.

Mum pushes a piece of salmon around her plate.

"I promise."

Mum looks at me, eyes brimming, and gives one tense nod.

Maybe she'll calm down enough to not hate me over Christmas.

Later, when I'm lying in bed, my phone vibrates beside me. I look at it in surprise. I wasn't expecting to hear from Mina so soon, and I haven't exactly been handing my number around.

It's Alex.

"Hey!" the message says. "Here's the video from the other day. You look like a pro."

I press play. He's actually right. When I landed it I'd thought it was really sketchy, but in the video it's practically graceful as I grind along the rail on my back truck and pop neatly back to the ground, balancing with my arms as Alex starts whooping and the video cuts out.

Another message appears: "Also I asked and it's OK for me to have a plus one to Elena's New Year's party. Will you come?"

Of course I can't go to Elena's party with Alex. I'm attending it with Mina. And as a girl.

But then that feeling starts bubbling up again. The desire to do something reckless. I imagine a version of my life where I'm just Jay, who wears boys' clothes and skateboards and goes to a fun party with their friend Alex. Of course going with Mina will be fun too. Anything's fun with Mina. But I'll spend all night tugging at whatever outfit I choose, feeling like it's too short or too tight, avoiding looking at mirrors so I don't have to think about how much my hair makes me look like a girl. I want the world where I'm the Jay Alex knows, where I'm myself and do what I want instead of doing what my mother wants, like a superhero. Or an adult. Or just someone who isn't desperate for their mother's approval, I don't know. What would that Jay say?

I type "Nice, let's do it!" and smile, imagining I could just send that. Then I lock my phone and put it down. I go to sleep imagining I'm the Jay I want to be, with skateboarding posters all over my walls and clothes that I like hanging in my wardrobe.

The next day I wake up to a text from Alex. "Sick! So glad you can come". No. No no. I open the phone. Yep. I sent the text. I spend the next five minutes screaming into my pillow. Obviously I shouldn't even IMAGINE having nice things.

Jamie and I go play catch in the back garden. I'm wearing a fluffy peach jumper. Mum chose it. Of course. I feel like a prize poodle with a terrible secret to reveal.

"Jamie," I say, as we throw a tennis ball back and forth, "I may have done something unwise last night."

"*How?*" he asks. "You were in your room the whole time. Weren't you? Did you sneak out? Why didn't you invite me?"

"I didn't sneak out. I sent an unwise text."

"Saying what?"

"Saying that I'd go to Elena's New Year's Eve party."

"You were already going to that."

"I told *Alex* I'd go."

He looks at me for a second before he realizes what I'm saying.

"OH. Oh my god. That is unwise."

"I know."

"Why did you do that?"

"I didn't mean to! After Sad Mum happened I just

151

couldn't stop thinking about how much I wanted to be able to go to the party as myself, so I wrote out a text that I would send if that was possible, because it felt good to pretend, and then I didn't send it but I accidentally did. OK, it doesn't sound like it makes a lot of sense now that I'm saying it out loud, but…"

"How would a homeschooled, religious child even know about Elena's party?"

"Alex invited me."

Jamie stares at me.

"Stop staring at me."

"I don't get it. Alex doesn't talk to *anybody* at school. He walks around with headphones in, he reads a book at lunchtime, and he skateboards away as fast as he can at the end of the day. Girls are always trying to talk to him, and he doesn't even look at them. Why is he inviting you to parties?"

"Look, I don't get it, either! I guess he likes me because I skate. You know what skatepark friendships are like, you spend a lot of time together."

"Why do I feel like you're lying to me?"

Because right now, I'm lying to everyone about something?

"I'm not."

"I don't believe you."

I drop the tennis ball. I feel like he's slapped me. Me and Jamie have always trusted each other completely. Always. But he's right. I am lying to him. I wish I could stop lying.

I wish I could even tell Mum the truth. Well, about how I want to look – not about Alex. That one's not really Parent Information. Even telling Ms George a bit of the truth made me feel lighter and safer. Imagine how much better I'd feel if I could just be honest with everybody?

I should tell him the truth.

But what would he say? "Just tell Alex the truth too, he'll like you for who you are!" like we're in a Pixar movie or something. Life isn't like that, and he only thinks it is because he doesn't understand what it's like for people to think something's wrong with you. So instead I pick up the tennis ball and throw it as hard as I can at the fence behind him, making him jump.

"Fine, then. *Don't*."

CHAPTER 13

THE TOP FIVE REASONS THIS CHRISTMAS IS TERRIBLE

1. Jamie is angry at me.
2. Mum is sad.
3. That's my whole family out of sorts.
4. Mum gets Jamie a pair of trainers that I asked her for last year. She gets me a turquoise bodycon dress.
5. Jamie opens the cream Quiksilver hoodie and the video game he's wanted for months that I've got him, nods once and says, "Thanks."

That's it. He gets me a book of historic photos of Hatch Heath. I know he can't give me anything related to my real hobbies in front of Mum, but it still feels weirdly impersonal.

On Boxing Day morning, I head for the skatepark. Alex is already there, riding what looks like a new board.

"Hey!" I say as I ride up. "Let me see."

He grins and pushes the board across the ground to me so I can check it out.

"Nice," I say appreciatively. "Who gave you this?"

"My dad."

"Seriously?"

He blushes and goes quiet, but I know his dad giving him this is a big deal.

"Alex, that's great. Is he being nicer to you?"

"Um, actually, yeah."

"Well, come on, tell me more," I say, sitting down on my board to listen to him.

"OK ... so, I came home a few weeks back, and he was on my laptop."

"That's normally a very bad sign."

"I know, right? But he was watching videos I have of me skating. When I came in, he said, 'You're really good at this, aren't you?' And since then ... I don't know, it's like he suddenly *gets it*. He says he's proud of me for being so 'dedicated'."

"That's amazing!" I jump up and give him a hug. It's the first time I've done that, and while I'm doing it, I realize it's more something Mina's-friend-Jay would do than something Alex's-friend-Jay would do. But he puts his arms around me straight away. I can feel his bicep on my shoulder and smell a new body spray he's wearing. He must have got it for Christmas.

"Yeah, it's cool," he says as we break apart. "Next thing I knew he was letting me pick out a skateboard for Christmas."

"You're living the dream, my man."

He blushes again (he's really blushing a lot today), then starts rummaging in his backpack.

"He actually let me get something extra," he says, "and I didn't want it, so, like, you can have it."

He takes out a box of new wheels and hands them to me. I know as soon as I see them that he bought them for me himself. I mentioned that I needed new ones, like, a month ago, and told him my favourite wheels were from the company Alien Workshop. These are a new model and I know they weren't cheap.

"Alex. Oh my god."

"If you don't want them I'll take them," he says quickly.

"This is the best Christmas present anybody's given me this year."

He grins, looking adorably sheepish, kicking his feet against the ground and taking his hands in and out of his pockets. "Oh. Well. Good."

"I can't believe I didn't get you anything!"

"Nah, it's not like that. I just thought you might like them."

"I *love* them."

"Cool."

"I'm totally going to get you something back."

"You don't have to."

"I want to. I just didn't know we were, like, Christmas-present-type friends. But I'm really glad we are."

"I'm glad you're coming to that party with me. It would suck otherwise."

I want to make up an excuse about the party right there and then ... but he's already started skating.

I think we've probably hit Alex's emotional limit.

For the next few days, me and Jamie aren't really speaking. But we're working together nonetheless, because we're slowly introducing Mum to the idea of us attending Elena's party.

This is a delicate process that we've got very good at over the years. You can't start it too far in advance because she'll have too much time to think about everything that could go wrong and go back on her agreement.

So instead we do the following: we breadcrumb.

"Jamie, have you heard about Elena's New Year's Eve party?"

"Oh, yeah, Elena's party, everyone is going."

"Her parents are so nice, and they know all about the party."

"Her older brother will be there to keep an eye on things."

We don't overdo it, or explicitly ask to go yet, and I'm testing the waters when I ask to stay at Mina's on the twenty-ninth. I guessed right that Mum would approve, even if things are still tense in the house; she likes Mina too much to say no.

To be honest, I think a night away from her and Jamie is exactly what I need.

"Welcome to my humble abode," Mina says when she swings the door open, wearing an annoyingly cool dark purple tracksuit combo, the jacket unzipped over a white T-shirt. There are lighter strands mixed into her braids now, and it really suits her. I don't know why, because I wouldn't wear the stuff she wears, but I love looking at her outfits.

"This abode is not humble," I say. "I thought this was flats, not a house of its own."

The hallway is warmly lit by trendy, industrial-looking lamps and on the walls there's art consisting of colourful, abstract shapes. I hover in front of a painting of a triangle that catches my eye. Why does it look so *interesting*? It's a triangle. At the end of the hall I can see floor-to-ceiling windows in a gleaming kitchen and hear her parents talking.

"We can dissect my privilege another time," Mina says, leading me in. "Come meet Mum and Dad."

Mina's parents are awesome, like I knew they would be. Her dad doesn't say much, but he's always smiling, and when he does speak his voice is low and resonant. Mina's mum looks *so* much like Mina and is constantly laughing — at something Mina's said, at something I've said, at something she's said. She's dressed like she's going out even though she isn't, and I can totally see where Mina gets her looks and style from.

"Jay, come down and hang out with us if you get bored of each other! Or I'll come up and hang out with you, if I get bored of him," her mum teases, poking her dad playfully.

He gasps and flounces away in mock outrage, and she chases after him, giggling.

"They're so cool!" I whisper as Mina takes me upstairs.

"You can go back down if you want," she says. "I'll go watch the movie by myself."

"No way. What are we watching?"

"A horror movie."

"I hate horror movies."

"That's not going to change the plan, I'm afraid."

"That's not a very respectful way to treat your *guest*."

"But *do* I respect my guest? They're too scared to watch a horror movie."

"I did NOT say I was scared."

"Look, if you need me to hold your hand you can just ask."

I glance at her hand on the banister, at her purple nails (does she repaint them every day to match her outfits??) and feel myself turn red. The image of us shrieking at the movie and her grabbing my hand makes me feel like I'm dangling at a great height for a second. I blink the image away.

"Unfortunately, I'm very tough. I've never been scared before and I don't plan to start now. What else is on the agenda, then?"

"I have a small bottle of vodka."

"You weren't kidding about cocktails."

"No, I was not. I'm very disappointed you didn't bring the trench coat you promised me."

"How did you get it?"

"Borrowed from my parents' collection, via outright stealing. I also have a large bottle of Coke, obtained via legal purchase. We are going to drink them, order a pizza, bitch about school, and see where the night takes us."

"What if I'm a bad drunk?"

"I'll send you home."

Her room is up in the attic, where it feels like we're totally hidden away. She has a huge double bed and loads of beanbags and cushions on the floor to slump on. There's a lot of pink and purple going on, which I wouldn't normally like, but even I have to say it's tastefully done.

We barely pay attention to the movie as we start chatting

and drinking. It's a really small bottle, and it doesn't make me feel that different. Though it does make me feel a little bit like I do when Mum is getting to be too much for me and I'm starting to feel rebellious: like I want to do something a bit wild, just to see what happens. Mina's about the same as she always is, just gigglier than normal. I notice that both of us seem to be slouching and leaning back. Like we're relaxing in front of each other for the first time.

"Jay, can I put make-up on you?" she asks.

"Ick. OK, but only as a joke. Oh! And you have to take a picture so I can show my mum; she'll love it."

"Right on track for my next question. Amazing. It's barely eight o'clock." She starts taking a huge collection of pots and brushes out of a drawer. "Tell me what the deal is with your mum."

"Fine…" I'd sort of resigned myself before I came over to telling her a bit more. Not everything, but more.

She scooches around so she's sitting directly in front of me and our crossed legs are touching. I jolt slightly. I glance up to see if she's noticed that we're really *quite extremely close*, but she's busy taking things out of a make-up bag. Maybe this is just a normal way that friends sit, even if it makes me feel like my stomach is jumping around inside my body.

"You told me that she didn't like you doing 'boyish' things, right?"

"Yeah." I flinch back as she brings something near my eye.

"It's eyeliner not knives, Jay. Relax." She's so close to my face, it makes me want to giggle.

"Well, you've probably guessed that I'm more of, like, a tomboy, or whatever you want to call it."

"I thought as much. So explain to me why you're currently wearing a pink skirt."

"Mum bought it for me and she wanted me to wear it." I pause, trying to work out the best way to explain it all. "When we moved here, I told Mum I'd try to be different. More like a girl."

"But why?"

"She never liked how I dressed before. And then at my last school there was a bit of good-fashioned bullying. But it got pretty bad."

"So bad you had to move?"

"I guess."

I think about it for a second. That was why we had to move ... right? Obviously I got hurt badly, and that was awful, and then Mum totally lost it.

And it was all because of me. Right?

She stops wiping a powdery thing over my eyelids and leans back to look at me. "I'm sorry. That's horrible."

"Yeah, it wasn't great. I don't really like talking about it."

"It's OK. You don't have to say anything else."

I smile. "Have I revealed enough of my secrets to reassure you that we're friends, then?"

"Yes. And someday I'll make you tell me everything. When you've *finally* got over your trauma," she says with a dramatic eye roll, cracking me up. She leans in again and starts tickling my cheeks with a brush. "It doesn't seem right for her to stop you dressing how you want, though."

"Well, hang on, you've never seen what I looked like before. I might have looked horrible," I joke.

"Mm, I bet you didn't, though. What kind of thing did you like wearing?"

"Jeans, T-shirts, sneakers … but, you know, *boys'* jeans. Boys' clothes."

"I'd like to see you dressed like that," she says, smiling.

I should have trusted Jamie from the start. Mina really is the coolest. Maybe I'm a little too inclined to pessimism.

Pessimistically, I don't tell her I want my hair cut like a boy, though. That feels like a detail too far. That would tip me over from "tomboy" into "looks like a guy".

"So are you gonna tell me more about you and Dani?"

"Absolutely," she says, putting something on my lips, "once we've finished the vodka. Now, look upon my works!" she says dramatically, grabbing a mirror and holding it up.

I glance at the person in the glass and crack up. She's given me a cool, smoky look with long eyelashes and black eyeshadow around my eyes. I look ridiculous. Mum will love it.

"Fantastic," I say, handing her my phone to take a picture. "Can't wait to show Mum, she'll be delighted."

"Do you like it?"

"I respect your skill, but no. Do you?"

She puts one hand in my hair to push it back and looks at me appraisingly. I feel my breath catch while she does it and stay very still.

"You have a really good bone structure. And excellent eyebrows. You're really good-looking."

"Thanks?" My face is burning up.

"But this is not really your 'look', that much is obvious."

I nod in agreement. She takes her hand out of my hair and hands me a make-up wipe. I finally breathe out. We wash our faces and brush our teeth and put on pyjamas. When we're back in her room together the room feels … not *awkward*, exactly, but kind of tense in a nice way. We make eye contact and neither of us says anything.

I break almost immediately.

"Tell me about Dani!" I blurt out.

"Ahhhh, fine. Get into bed."

I look around the room like more beds will appear. "This bed?"

"Do you see another bed?"

"Sorry, I just didn't think I'd be sleeping in your bed."

"Would you like me to show you to the spare room, Your Highness?"

"*No*," I say. She's totally enjoying my awkwardness.

I climb into the bed and lie on my back like a plank on the extreme edge of the mattress. She laughs and turns off the light. I hear the duvet rustling as she climbs into the bed on the other side. She sighs.

"This is actually quite a weird situation to tell you this in."

"Oh good, it's not just me who thinks it's weird."

She laughs softly. My eyes haven't adjusted yet. Her laugh comes from nowhere out of the darkness.

"So, this isn't a big deal, so don't make it one, OK?"

"OK."

"I'm bi," she says breezily. "It's not a big deal."

"It's not a big deal," I say back. But I can feel my heart beating faster. I haven't had a friend who isn't straight before.

"I'd told Dani that a few months before the party where things … went wrong. *She* said it wasn't a big deal too, but I could tell she thought it was a little strange. We used to have sleepovers all the time and suddenly I could see her glancing at me, like I was going to try to watch her changing or something. It annoyed me. I didn't like *her*. I've never even really liked a girl; I just know that I'm not straight. So yeah, it annoyed me."

"I bet."

"But by the time we went to Elena's last party together, I thought things had gone back to normal – we were having a good time, she was being mean to people, I was making

165

it seem like she was joking, our usual routine. So then someone suggested playing spin the bottle…"

Man. I thought city kids were meant to be cooler. It turns out everybody's been living it up in the countryside.

"Dani span it, and it landed on me. I said I didn't want to play any more, but she came over and kissed me. All the boys were cheering, and it made me so annoyed that *that* was the first time I kissed a girl. It was just a joke to her, but I wanted it to mean something to me, and have it be with someone I actually really wanted to kiss. I could tell she was only doing it because Alex was there. She dragged him into the game, and made him spin the bottle, and it landed on me."

I feel a huge rush of jealousy imagining Alex kissing Mina.

"She was glaring at me, but I was so annoyed at her, and it's just a game, right? So I pecked him for, like, half a second. That was it. After we left the party she flipped out on me. She was yelling at me that I was in love with her and that I kissed Alex to make her jealous, and that I was weird and obsessed with her, and … well, she said a lot of things. I should have known kissing Alex would make her switch, even if it was for a game. I should have known she'd be weird about the bi thing."

I've turned over on my side to face her. I think she's in the same position, though I can barely see her now in the moonlight coming in through the curtains.

166

"Why didn't you tell me?"

"I guess I was nervous it might change things with us, like it did with me and Dani. But I know you're not like that. In fact, are you…?"

She lets it hang in the air.

"Am I what?"

"Not to assume, with the whole tomboy thing…"

I laugh. "Am I gay?"

"Well, are you straight?"

"I don't know."

She doesn't answer. And suddenly I feel like I want to close the distance between us, somehow. Like I want to reach out for her, but I don't know why.

The silence stretches on.

"Mina?" I say. I have no idea what I'm going to say next.

She's asleep. Of course she's asleep.

Luckily, when I wake up the next day, the feeling is gone, neatly and safely crushed back into whatever box it came from. We're just Jay and Mina, laughing and teasing each other over her dad's excellent pancakes.

"How do you feel after your two glasses of alcohol?" she asks as she walks me down her driveway.

"Wonderful. It turns out I'm fantastic after a vodka and coke. Charming, I'd say."

"Don't let it go to your head."

"Too late."

"I'll see you for Elena's. Want to get ready together?"

I remember with a jolt that I need to cancel on Alex. I can't believe I didn't think about that at all while we were together.

"If Mum lets me go, definitely. But I'm not letting you put eyeshadow on me again."

"But you looked so *pretty*," she teases.

I pretend to flip my hair to make her laugh. Then we hug and I watch as she walks back inside.

The whole morning, we didn't mention what we spoke about the night before. But as I walk home, I can't stop thinking about it. Mina was brave enough to come out as bi to someone like Dani and again to me. Sure, Dani's not exactly been an ally, but maybe that's on her. I don't think any differently of Mina at all now that she's told me. Ms George was accepting and kind about the way I looked at my old school.

Maybe my luck's changing now that I know people like Mina and Ms George.

CHAPTER 14

I'm not feeling so lucky any more. I'm feeling … *anxious*, to say the least.

The New Year's Eve party's tonight, and I haven't cancelled on Alex yet.

I know. Look, it's hard being two people. Especially now that they're booked for the same event, with different friends. Even when I cancel on Alex, he might be there and think, "Boy, that girl sure reminds me of a certain home-educated skateboarder." A lot could go wrong. I actually thought I had an easy way out: Mum had such a Sad Mum moment recently I thought she wouldn't let me go to the party at all.

And then, yesterday, Mum sat down with me in the living room.

"I just wanted to say," she said (I was already nodding sagely, ready to accept that I couldn't go to the party), "that I do know how hard you're trying. I know it can't always be easy. But you've come so far and made so much effort to fit in, and made so many friends, and I *am* proud of you. I know you're going to try even harder next year. You should go have fun with Mina tomorrow on New Year's Eve."

It honestly took me about thirty seconds to stop staring at her blankly and say, "Oh, wow! Thanks!"

"And if you'd like to stay at Mina's again, go ahead. Her parents sound lovely, and it seemed like you had such a great time with your makeover!"

Honestly. The one time I *want* her to ground me, she's giving me more freedom than I've ever had. I should have made friends with a pretty girl years ago – Mum's letting me get away with murder.

So that brings us right up to today, with the party in several hours, and I guess I'm going. With Mina, of course. How could I ever have gone as boy Jay? Of course, this still leaves me with the risk of Alex recognizing girl Jay. Hopefully he's as uninterested in Heath Girls' students at parties as he is at school.

I find an outfit that I don't one hundred per cent hate – black leggings, black trainers, and a black T-shirt. Don't get me wrong, I don't *like* it – it's way too form-fitting. But at

170

least it's black. If I just pretend I'm purposefully dressing like a superhero, it feels a little bit better. Maybe I should get a cape. Actually, it's probably better not to give Dani too much ammo.

Sadly, I take out my phone to text Alex, wincing when I see he's already sent me the address for tonight. I've been avoiding it, but I know what I have to do.

"Hey, I'm really sorry," I type, "my mum won't let me go out." I add a sad face. And then delete it. It feels like a little much.

He replies almost instantly.

"Don't worry, I didn't really want to go anyway."

I hope he's not angry. But crisis averted, I guess. He's not going, either. No need to be worried – or this sad. I try to push away the thoughts of the evening we could have had, in a perfect world.

Before Mina arrives, I wander over to Jamie's room. Everything feels like such a mess at the moment, and I miss my brother.

"Jamie," I say, leaning around his door, "truce for the night? Come hang out with me and Mina while we get ready?"

He's lying on his bed wearing comfy joggers and a sweatshirt, playing the *Shoot 'Em Up* video game I bought him for Christmas. He pauses it when I walk in, like he doesn't want me to see that he's enjoying my gift. I can see him weighing up how annoyed he is with me versus how much he wants to hang out and gossip with Mina. He's a social animal, not the type to willingly pass up a chance to chat and shriek. And he and Mina are definitely similarly chatty and shrieky. They're going to get on like a house on fire. Not that that saying makes a lot of sense. Generally houses and fires are things that you want to keep separate. But these two are going to have so much fun gossiping that I can't wait to set their houses on fire. That's not a saying, is it? That's just a threat. I'm nervous. I just want Jamie to forgive me already.

"OK," he says finally.

"Really?"

"Yeah."

"We're OK?"

"For tonight, anyway. Yeah."

We do not sound OK.

"Do you like the video game?"

"It's all right."

God, he really isn't happy with me. It's shooting zombies, what's not to love?

"I'm sorry I've annoyed you so much," I say weakly.

"I just don't understand why you're being so secretive suddenly. You know you can say anything to me."

It's so much like what Mina said to me when we argued that I know I'm the problem. I wish I *could* tell him anything, but I just can't. Not when I've made so many odd choices. Me and my alter ego almost went to the same party tonight. I try to imagine what he would say if I *could* tell him everything.

"*Jamie, quick question. Why did I subconsciously tell Alex I would go to a party with all of my schoolmates while dressed as my secret identity?*"

We're back in the war room. Jamie is hunched over a desk with a map laid out on it, moving figurines around frantically.

"Well," he says, "I've looked at it from every possible angle."

"And what's your conclusion?"

"That you're ridiculous."

"Oh."

"Beyond ridiculous. You're so unhappy with how things are that you're being bizarre. You could have ended up in a room with Alex while dressed as a girl, why would you consider that a reasonable risk?"

"Uh … um, because…"

"Because you SHOULDN'T BE ALLOWED OUTSIDE, that's why!" he yells, sweeping the map off the table.

Jeez. He's even angry at me in my own imagination.

"Yes, I know I'm bad at being a person. But I just wanted to go with both of them so badly! And he's not even going, so it's fine."

He thinks hard.

"I've got a solution that would stop anything like this happening again, but you won't like it."

"Tell me."

"You could tell the truth. Tell Alex and Mina who you actually are."

I tell imaginary Jamie to shut up. I don't want to hear it. He should know how badly that could go. To real Jamie I just say sorry and look away.

The doorbell rings and I run to drag Mina through to my room with Jamie before she and Mum can chat too much. Luckily Mum is on the phone and doesn't come out of the living room.

Mina closes my door behind her and dramatically acts like she's checking the coast is clear. She takes a fancy-looking bottle labelled 'Buck's Fizz' out of her bag. Jamie whoops and sneaks to the kitchen to grab glasses.

"Another nefariously borrowed beverage from your parents' collection?" I ask.

"They actually *gave* me this," she says. "This beverage is parentally endorsed."

I stare at her. "God, they're cool."

Jamie comes back in and shuts the door.

Mina says, "I should probably point out at this stage that Buck's Fizz is essentially orange juice and there's barely any alcohol in it."

"Well, Jamie's only ever had non-alcoholic beer before, so it's a step up," I say, hoping he'll jump in on that funny anecdote with me.

"That's not true. Me and the Toms drink sometimes."

"The Toms?" I say in surprise.

He nods.

I try to ignore the feeling in my stomach I get because

he hasn't told me that. I barely know anything about his Toms.

Maybe I haven't really asked.

"Oooh, which Toms?" Mina asks.

"Davidson and Proctor," he answers.

"I kissed Tom Proctor at a party once," Mina says cheerily.

"I know, he talks about it literally all the time." They both cackle, practically in harmony.

"It was *a year* ago!" Mina shrieks. She pours them both a drink.

How am I *already* left out of this? They start chatting away about guys from the boys' school, a lot of whom seem to have crushes on Mina. I don't really know any of the guys, but I decide I don't like any of them.

I keep looking at my phone, hoping Alex will say something else.

"Oooh, who're you texting?" Mina asks.

"She'll never tell you," Jamie says, half joking. "She keeps her secrets."

"Doesn't Jay *love* to keep secrets?"

They both laugh, and I try to laugh along, even though it feels a bit pointed from both of them.

"Just checking the time," I lie.

Me and Jamie go change into our outfits for the night while Mina puts on her make-up in his mirror. Jamie's wearing basically the same thing as me – all black – but it looks so much better on him. So I decide not to look at any mirrors any more. Problem solved.

We finish the Buck's Fizz, which is basically just fun orange juice but is still very nice.

"Time to go!" Mina says, slipping the empty bottle back into her bag so Mum doesn't see it.

We say goodnight to Mum, who's going over to one of her new friend's houses.

"Girls, have a great night! Be safe. Jamie, let me know what time you'll be back." She smiles, but I can see she's pretty nervous. Still, this is kind of cool. She's actually trying to let us go out like other teenagers even though it scares her. I feel a rush of affection for her. Being her daughter is so confusing.

Still, as we walk to the party, I find myself wishing Mum had let the anxiety win and made me stay inside under her watchful gaze tonight. Going to a party in the clothes that I hate when I keep imagining the alternative is making me sad.

When we walk in, I can immediately tell this is a *good party*. Elena is rich. Like, *rich* rich. I thought Mina's house was big and this is basically twice the size. There's free food and drinks everywhere, and an actual professional DJ – albeit one who turns out to be Elena's older brother. He punctuates songs by yelling at people not to lean on the china cabinet, which me, Mina and Jamie really enjoy.

Yeah, it's a good party. Shame I'm too stressed about Alex to enjoy it.

Jamie's friends are there, and he introduces us.

"Mina, you already know Tom and Tom," he says. "Jay, meet the Toms. Toms, this is my sister."

Tom Proctor is tall and looks like he plays some kind of contact sport. He immediately starts talking to Mina. He's pretty clearly into her and evidently hanging on to hope from that kiss last year. I keep glancing over at them. I wonder if he's bothering her. Maybe I should go rescue her. I mean, she looks like she's having a pretty great time, laughing at his jokes and everything, but maybe she's just being polite … or maybe she really likes him. Which is fine too. I guess.

I'm standing in an old-fashioned TV studio in front of a live audience. Mina and Tom are waltzing together in the background.

"That's totally fine with me," I say, gesturing at them. "Why wouldn't that be fine?"

"AWWW," the audience choruses.

I glare at them, annoyed.

"What?! It's fine! I don't mind, it's not like I'm going to dance with her…"

"OOOOooo!"

"Shut up!"

"It's nice to finally meet you!" says Tom Davidson, snapping me out of it. He has chubby cheeks and little round glasses. He looks younger than he must be.

"You too," I say. "It's nice to meet the famous Toms. Has one of you ever considered getting a nickname?"

"People call me Little Tom," he says, "which might start to affect my ego eventually."

I laugh and notice Jamie has drifted slightly away from us to talk to Elena.

"Hey, would you like some of this beer?" Tom Davidson says, holding up a can and two plastic cups. I look around again. Jamie and Elena are laughing at something, Mina has her arm on Tom Proctor's arm and, you guessed it, they're also laughing at something. I feel a rush of jealousy. But whatever. It's fine. Everybody can laugh at whatever they want, in whatever pairs they like.

"Why don't people just call you Davidson?" I ask, holding the cups while he pours.

"Because there's another guy called Davidson in the year," he says.

"You're *kidding*. Are there no names left?"

He laughs again. Nice kid. But I start imagining another world, where I'm just the Jay that Alex knows.

Me and Alex meet each other on the street outside and slap each other on the shoulders before heading in together. We set our skateboards down by the door, next to other people's coats and bags.

"Kind of strange seeing you without a board," I joke as we walk into the house.

"Kind of strange seeing you without that hat on," Alex says.

I reach up and push a hand through my hair to muss it up. It's short like it used to be, with a tiny bit of wax in it to keep it messy.

"Alex!" Dani is waving at us as we step into the kitchen, though of course I don't know who she is.

"Hey, Dani," Alex says, "this is Jay."

Dani isn't rude to me, but she definitely only has eyes for Alex. When she goes to get a drink, Alex grabs my arm.

"C'mon, let's go before she comes back."

"Lovers' tiff?" I tease him as we sneak into the other room where it's darker and everyone's dancing.

"She's not my 'lover'." He laughs. "Who says 'lover'? She maybe does have a bit of a thing for me, though."

"Is that the curse of being unbearably handsome? You know most people don't have swathes of admirers, right?"

He laughs and playfully shoves me.

I look back at Tom and laugh at whatever it is he's just said. I take a sip of beer. Well, it actually tastes pretty horrible and has nothing on the Buck's Fizz, so I end up just holding it like a prop. Objectively I think beer might be a cooler drink of choice than Buck's Fizz, but I'm willing to accept the Buck's Fizz loving side of myself.

Eventually we rejoin Jamie and Mina. Jamie is now occasionally putting his arm around Elena, who is beaming at him with that look he sometimes gets from girls, like everything he says is the funniest thing ever. It's annoying. I know from experience that only about ninety per cent of what he says is actually funny. *No one has a perfect hit rate.*

I talk to Tom Proctor a little bit, in between his adoring gazes at Mina. I don't like him. Not for any particular reason, I just do not. He's too tall, or something. He has one of those bodies that looks like a letter V, where it's like, *we get it! You've had puberty! Chill out! No, I'm not jealous!*

"How are you enjoying your first party?" Mina teases me when her Tom goes to get her a drink.

"I don't know where you're getting your information from, Mina. I've been to other parties."

"My mistake. How are you enjoying your second party?"

"It's really cool. And you know what, I think it's especially good because I haven't seen Dani once."

"Right?! Nothing makes a party like not receiving any withering blows to your self-esteem."

"Well, it's early yet. She's probably still prepping put-downs. Actually, I wonder where she is."

"Hiding in the walls, waiting for the best moment to say something mean. Nah, she's probably off trying to get Alex to kiss her." Ugh.

"I don't think he's coming," I say, and then realize I shouldn't know that and change the subject. "Speaking of kissing…" I say, leaning in towards her to whisper.

"Are you coming on to me?" she teases, wiggling her eyebrows around.

I pause, mid-lean, realizing that it looks like I am. Unintentionally. Of course. "No way, I don't think I could take Big Tom."

Mina smirks.

"Seems like you and him ... get on pretty well."

"He's cool."

I'm just about to ask her outright if she likes him when the Toms come back, which is probably a good thing, because I suddenly feel like I don't want to know.

"Guess I'll see you later then," Mina says, with a teasing wave.

I watch her walk back over to Tom. It's fine; obviously, she can like whoever she wants. Maybe I'm just used to having all of her attention to myself or something.

"Excuse me, I'm just gonna go find the bathroom," I tell my Tom.

"Do you want me to come with you?"

"To the bathroom, Tom?"

He looks horribly embarrassed. "Oh no. I meant to show you where it is. I'll stop talking for ever."

We both laugh. I'm glad my brother is friends with him, he's a cool kid.

I slip through the crowd and head upstairs. I keep glancing sadly at the people around me, feeling like they're themselves in a way that I'm not. I pass a boy and a girl sitting against a wall, laughing and sharing a can. I imagine me and Alex there instead.

We're laughing about a bail I had last week, and feeling pleasantly invisible as people walk past. A blonde girl walks by and Alex glances at her nervously.

"Don't worry," I tease him, "it's not your lover Dani."

"You've got to stop calling her that." He grins.

"So how come you don't like her back?"

"I don't know, I just don't. I feel like I don't always like the stuff I'm supposed to like."

"Is that a riddle?"

He's starting to turn red, but he's not avoiding eye contact with me.

"Do you know what I mean?" he asks, slowly. "Are you the same?"

The countdown starts and we keep staring at each other...

The countdown to midnight starts while I search for the bathroom. Ah, the perfect time to be alone in a hallway. I shake myself out of my ridiculous daydream when I round a corner and see him. On the other side of the room, Alex has a tight smile on his face; he's sipping a drink and not joining in with the chanting.

Dani is next to him, screaming the last few numbers out. She looks incredible, as much as I hate to admit it. She's wearing a tight black dress and there's dark eyeshadow around her eyes. Her and Alex match. They look *right*, standing next to each other. So when she turns on her high heels and kisses him, it makes perfect sense that his arms slip around her waist. A few of Dani's minions nearby squeal, like their two favourite characters in a movie have finally ended up together. It looks totally cinematic. They're both beautiful. They're in the glow of a string of fairy lights. It's perfect.

I turn around and walk out. I text Jamie quickly: "Not feeling well. Going home. Don't worry." He'll tell Mina.

I storm across town, my breath clouding up in front of me, trying not to cry. Useless. What did I think would happen tonight? That Alex and I would be the ones kissing? Ridiculous. I know that Mum's still at her friend's house, so I barge into the dark house noisily, change into my skating clothes and grab my skateboard. I'm doing *one* thing that makes me happy tonight, even if the ground is frosty and it's pitch black.

I skate to the park as fast as I can. The street lamps cast just enough light to see. I bomb up and down the ramps, popping as high as I can and stomping back down to the ground on all my tricks. When I bail I just get back up and go again, even when it hurts. I can feel a graze on my arm starting to bleed and I'm panting for breath, but I don't care. I could do this all night, to stop myself thinking about all the picture-perfect couples I look nothing like. Mina and Tom Proctor. Jamie and Elena. Alex and Dani.

Something shoves me in the side and sends me spinning against the concrete side of a ramp.

I hear, "What the *hell*?"

I'm so shocked that I don't say anything for several seconds, just stare at Alex with my mouth open and my eyes wide. He kicks his skateboard across the ground.

"You're *here*? Seriously? You went to the skatepark instead?"

He shoves me again. I should be scared. He's bigger and taller than me, and he has me cornered. Instead I'm angry. All I can see is his arms going round Dani's waist and him kissing her back.

"Back off, Alex."

"Why would you lie about not being allowed out?"

"I said back off."

"Are you *mad at me*? Why the hell are YOU mad at ME?" He's really yelling now.

"What do you care if I didn't come to your ... atheist party?" I snap.

"I invited you! Of course I care! You're the ... you're the one who doesn't care!"

"What do *you* care?"

We have got to stop saying care.

"Why would I have asked if I didn't care?"

"You didn't look like you cared when you were kissing that girl!"

He blinks. It got out before I could stop it.

"Wait — you were there?" His voice softens.

"Yeah, I was there!" I yell back, feeling like I have the

upper hand now. "I came to find you. And then I left because you were obviously busy."

"What do you care if I was kissing a girl?"

Ah. He's got me there.

"I … I don't… Who said I cared?"

The rush of adrenaline I feel makes my stomach turn, because I can see the realization in his eyes. He knows now. That pathetic denial was as good as a confession. He knows exactly why his religious buddy would have sprinted out of a party when Dani kissed him. I feel like we're floating in space, suspended in complete silence. I feel completely vulnerable. I realize how close he is. I want to run away. Push him away.

I want to kiss him.

And then he steps forward and kisses *me*.

At first I can't believe it's happening. His lips are pressed against mine so gently. He has one hand resting on the side of my face. It's so soft, but it feels like an electric shock. I don't know how long we stay like that. He pulls back and looks at me. For some reason we both start laughing. He pulls me against him in a rough hug, like he does when I've landed a trick I've been working on for ages.

"Hey," he says, so quietly I almost miss it, "please don't tell anyone."

"About … this?"

That's got to be a bad sign, someone swearing you to secrecy after your first kiss.

"That I'm gay."

Oh.

Well, that clears that up: he definitely thinks I'm a guy.

CHAPTER 15

I skate home feeling on top of the world.

I know this situation is actually incredibly complicated, but everything *feels* perfect right now. All my problems can wait until tomorrow. *Tonight I kissed the first person I've ever liked.*

As I approach our street, I pop my board up into the air and catch it, running quickly and carefully towards the house. I can see a light on upstairs in Mum's room. I'll change, then pretend I've just come home instead of going to Mina's because I wasn't feeling well. I use the shadows close to the house to sneak up to my window.

For the second time tonight, someone crashes into me.

I have GOT to be more aware of my surroundings. I topple to the ground, barely managing not to scream.

"Good luck explaining this one," a voice hisses.

"*Mina?*"

She's crouched above where I'm sprawled in the grass.

"Yes, it's Mina. Who did you think it was?"

"I don't know, some sort of murderer?"

"Then why didn't you scream?"

"I didn't want to get in trouble!"

"How scared of your mother *are* you? You would have preferred to be *murdered?*"

"Not *preferred,* but—"

"Shut up and start talking."

"Kind of a contradiction, Mina."

"Then shut up and start listening. Put yourself in my shoes. I realize my best friend has ditched the party we're at. Her brother says she's texted saying she's feeling unwell and is going home. I run after her, because I assume something is very wrong. I watch her go into her house, and a boy comes out. It takes me a second to work out that *she's* the boy."

I sit up on my elbows. Mina stares at my outfit, the hat my hair is tucked up under. I can't read her expression. I know Mina's an open-minded person, but pulling off a dramatic quick change in front of someone isn't exactly the gentlest way to reveal how you like to present, so I'm pretty nervous.

"Please don't tell me you followed her to the skatepark."

"That's exactly where I followed her, and found her *making out with the hottest guy in town*."

"I thought he wasn't your type."

"He's not, but I have eyes, I've seen the cheekbones. And stop trying to distract me. You need to explain what's going on, right now."

"OK, OK … but first I need you to stop whisper-yelling at me before my mother sees me dressed like this."

She thinks for a moment. I think she's genuinely considering getting me into more trouble but decides against it.

"All right. You can still stay at mine. You can borrow some clothes for the morning."

I nod because something tells me she's not taking no for an answer. I hide my board in the bush outside my window and she hauls me down the street. We walk back to hers at an abnormally fast pace, our breath misting in the freezing air, not speaking. I'm completely exhausted. All I want to do is go to bed and think about that kiss. What I don't want is to get yelled at by Mina, which is where it seems like my night is going.

She still doesn't say a single word as we enter and wave to her parents in the living room, who are busy with a group of friends, listening to music and clinking champagne glasses together, so they just beam at us without noticing their daughter is *furious*. She *still* doesn't say anything as we make our way up to her room. I send Mum a quick text to say that I'm back at Mina's and she replies with a smiley face. At least I'm not in trouble with her. After she shuts the bedroom door, Mina puts her hands on her hips and glares at me. "OK. Explain."

"I just … I just borrow Jamie's clothes when I go skateboarding, so that no one recognizes me if they see me."

"Right, sure, sure. And where does kissing Alex come into that?"

"Things may have got a little out of hand."

Her eyes go wide. "Wait. Does … Alex think you're a *boy*?"

"He – uh, yes."

"Jay, that's really messed up! Seriously. You're lying to him about something huge."

"I know, I know. Well, sort of. It's complicated. I wasn't *completely* sure he thought I was a boy until tonight. People don't always think I am one even when I'm dressed like this, but after he kissed me, he did say 'please don't tell anyone that I'm gay' so I think now it's pretty safe to say that he *does* think I'm a guy…"

Mina cuts off my rambling. "Oh my god. Alex is gay?"

"You can't tell anyone that."

"Obviously, but that's *fantastic*. Dani has been hurling herself at a gay guy *for years*!"

"Yeah, I also found that pretty funny."

"But back to the point. How long has this thing with Alex been going on?"

"There is no thing! Or at least there wasn't till tonight. We've just been skating together. Tonight I left the party and went to the park and he was there and ... he kissed me."

"This doesn't seem right, Jay."

I swallow. "But it doesn't feel like a lie."

Mina stares at me. "What do you mean?"

"OK, some of it feels like a lie; he thinks I'm a homeschooled religious kid. But the way I look, and the skating, and the things we have in common — *those* aren't lies. And even ... that he thinks I'm a boy. That doesn't quite feel like a lie, either. Does that make sense?"

Mina sits down slowly on the end of her bed, thinking.

"Are you going to tell him?" I ask nervously.

"No," she says, "you're my best friend. That means I keep your secrets."

"And I keep yours," I say.

"Easy for you to say. I don't have any secrets of quite this size."

I sit next to her on the bed. "Look, we've just kissed one time. We might not even talk again."

"You really like him, don't you?" she says.

I can't quite work out her expression. Maybe she's just annoyed about me not telling Alex everything as soon as he kissed me. Maybe she looks kind of sad. And for a second, in a way I don't really understand, I'm sad too. For some reason the image of her and Tom Proctor laughing together jumps into my head. One thing's for sure: it's absolutely time to come clean about everything.

"Yeah, I do."

Now she looks worried. "Jay, what do you think is going to happen here? That he's never going to find out?"

"No, of course not. I … I just…" I trail off, trying to put my thoughts into words. "I would like to tell Alex the truth. I think I should. It's just, tonight … he *liked* me, looking like this. It was nice, it felt right."

Mina looks even more worried, but she nods.

"Please be careful, Jay," she says. "Or else someone is going to get hurt. You need to tell him."

"I know."

And I mean it, I really do. When she goes to the toilet, I even pick up my phone. But there's a text from Alex: "I've wanted to kiss you for a really long time."

Smiling, I type back: "Me too."

The next morning, Mina and I wake up, and she lends me some clothes.

"So, you're going to tell Alex the truth?"

I nod. "I'll do it next time I see him in the skatepark. Doing it over text feels wrong."

She nods back. "Listen, I don't want to add to what I'm sure is already your very inflated ego…"

"So inflated. I'm officially hotter than Dani Hex."

"I wouldn't say that's what this proves. But you looked really good in your brother's clothes."

Despite everything, that keeps me smiling all the way home.

Mum is actually in a good mood when I walk in. If only I was in less personal turmoil myself, I could enjoy it more.

"Good morning!" she says brightly, holding out a tray of warm croissants.

I take one.

"What a cute T-shirt! Is it Mina's?"

"Yes, I forgot to bring a change. How was your night?"

"Lovely! Me and the ladies got a little tipsy and watched the fireworks. How was yours?"

"It was great! Elena's brother has DJ decks, so he played all the music. And it was nice to meet Jamie's friends from the boys' school."

But suddenly Mum sighs and looks down at her croissants. I wonder what they did.

"That's great. I know I can be a little … uptight with you and Jamie," she says, catching me totally by surprise, "but I think you're both growing up, and I should let go a little. I'm proud of you for being so responsible. I'm glad you had fun."

She smiles shyly, and for a second I want to throw my skateboard away for ever and get blonde highlights or something. She's really trying to change for me – maybe it's fair that I try to change for her.

"Here," she says, holding out the tray, "could you take Jamie a croissant?"

I slide one on to a plate and go upstairs, where I knock on his door. He's sprawled across the bed wearing clean clothes, looking immaculate, but he moans when I come in. "Feeling fresh, bro?"

"Not remotely. I've just been lying here completely still and then pretending to read a book every time Mum knocks."

"Did you have fun last night? Mina's great, right?"

"Yeah, she is. It was a good party."

The awkwardness is back.

"I'm sorry I left without saying anything."

"It's fine. I'm not going to bother asking why; I know you won't tell me."

I want to. But now I can't tell him the truth without revealing Alex's secret, and I feel like I owe Alex the truth first. It's like I'm in a Jenga tower of lies, and to be honest I don't want to knock it over. So I just stand there in silence.

Jamie turns away and goes back to pretending to read.

CHAPTER 16

For the next week it's weirdly hard to get hold of Alex. Not that I'm overthinking it. I'm thinking about it the correct amount. Why, hypothetically, would you send someone (me) the most romantic text that they (I) have ever received and then not reply to their (my) questions about when you'll be at the skatepark? Maybe he's confused. Coming out can't be easy, especially in the middle of the night when it's really cold. But I want to see him, because whatever happens, it's time to tell him everything about who I really am. Every day I go to the skatepark early in the morning and spend the rest of the day sitting in my house while Jamie keeps being awkwardly tense around me, barely tuning into conversation with Mum, texting Mina about what Alex might be thinking.

The day before school starts again, he's finally there when I roll up to the skatepark. My heart jumps, and for a second I'm *so* excited to reach into my backpack and pull out the present I've been carrying for him since it arrived a few days ago, hoping to see him. It's a book about the history of skateboarding called *The Answer Is Never*. I feel like I've really nailed that gift, to be honest. Does he like reading? Yes, he does. Does he like skateboarding? Evidently. I've crushed it. I'm just about to say all of that, when I notice the way he freezes when he sees me.

"Hey," I say, "how's it going?"

"I'm OK," he says, and starts skating again, not looking at me. Oh.

"Yeah? Are you OK?" I say.

"Yeah," he says, still not looking at me.

OK, I'm not going to claim to be the world's most communicative guy, but there has to be a limit.

"Should we talk about New Year's Eve? There's something I need to tell you," I say.

He slows to a halt and takes a breath.

"Alex!" For a second I think I'm just having some sort of nightmarish hallucination, but no. I definitely know that voice.

Dani Hex is walking towards us, waving. Waving at Alex – she doesn't even glance at me. I pull my hat down lower over my face. Just before I yank it down, Alex's eyes flick to mine. He looks scared.

My adrenaline spikes. I'm barely three metres away from Dani, who has a very high chance of being able to recognize me. To get out of the skatepark I'd have to walk straight past her, because she's standing by the gate. The closer I am, the more dangerous this is. I'll wait, give it a few minutes and leave as unsuspiciously as possible. Which means not hurling myself over the fence and booking it. I try not to look at them and focus on skating. But most importantly listening. Maybe this isn't what I think it is, maybe she's just made the unexpected decision to get into skateboarding.

"What are you doing here?" mutters Alex.

"I think you mean, 'Hi, babe, great to see you'," Dani says with a nervous laugh.

God. He sure knows how to make a girl feel special. I can't help feeling bad for her. For a second.

"You said you were going to come skateboard here early today, so I thought I'd come watch you. Because I'm a supportive girlfriend, right?"

Well. There it is.

"Uh – yeah, right."

I pop a little backside 180 ollie on the quarter pipe and steal a glance at them. Dani has moved away from the gate and over to Alex. She pops up on her tiptoes and kisses him on the cheek. He shoots another panicked glance my way, looking mortified when he realizes that I've seen the kiss. I kickflip over the funbox as angrily as I can. Dani puts her bag down and sits down on the grind box.

"Go on," she says, "show me some tricks."

I take the opportunity to roll through the gate and start skating away from them. I don't say anything to Alex as I go. But I hear one more thing as I leave:

"Who's that? I've never seen him before."

"He's just some kid."

I sneak back into the house in a state of shell shock, almost forgetting to change into my normal clothes. Not that it really matters, because there's no *way* I'm coming out of my room for a good while.

I write out a text to Mina.

"So I just saw Alex at the skatepark, and Dani was there too. Looks like they're going out."

I'm about to send another message when my phone rings. It's Mina.

"Oh god. I'm sorry, Jay. Are you all right?"

"Wow, I feel like you phoned me before that text had even arrived. Fastest draw in the West."

"The tone of that text was eerily calm; I'm unsettled," she says.

"I am also unsettled."

"Seriously … are you OK?"

Am I? I flop back on my bed. It's kind of hard to say. So I start making jokes.

"Oh, I'm fine. As much as it pains me to see Dani get something that she wants."

Mina matches my tone instantly. "It really couldn't have happened to a worse person."

"I wonder if her boyfriend's mentioned that he's gay yet."

"Maybe he's saving that for an anniversary. Though, to be fair, he doesn't seem to fully grasp what the word means."

"Yeah, maybe he was reaching for 'bisexual' and didn't have the time for all those syllables."

"That's why most of us say 'bi'."

"Thank god I have the head of the community on the phone."

By the end of the call, we're both laughing, and I feel a little better. Mina makes me promise to call her if I'm sad but keeps telling me I'm better off. And maybe she's right. I take out my phone and start deleting our texts. I'll just forget him. But I can't help keeping the text he sent on New Year's, about wanting to kiss me. One thing keeps playing on my mind – that thing Mum said to me, after what happened at my last school. "Who's going to be attracted to you if you keep looking like this?" It hurt then, but now, this feels like … evidence. Of course he actually wanted a pretty girl like Dani (I HATE complimenting Dani, even in my own thoughts). Alex is the person in this town who has seen me being most like myself, even if he thinks I'm an unusually small and high-pitched boy. And that's not what he wants. I don't call Mina, but I do start crying.

SPRING

CHAPTER 17

Me and Mina are sitting on a bench just outside the canteen. We're both wearing just our white school shirts with the sleeves rolled up, and the trees outside the windows have pink blossoms on them. Mina is wearing gold, slightly dangly earrings in the shape of leaves. Behind her, posters are up for the Summer Dance: "The Pink and Blue Dance: Only 1 Term to Go!" Over the last few weeks, I feel like we've got even closer, with her being so supportive over everything that happened with Alex. We chat on the phone most nights, and only partly about my disastrous love life. Love life is a pretty strong term for it, actually, but I don't know if there *is* a term for "gender-and-sexuality-bending-situation-where-we-kissed-once-but-he-has-a-girlfriend-now-and-never-comes-to-the-skatepark-any-more". Mostly we talk about other stuff. How things with me and Jamie are OK, but just not like they used to be. An argument she had with her mum about wearing a lower cut top when they went to her grandma's for lunch. (Her mum's stance was that the top is fine but not grandma-suitable; Mina's stance was that grandma needs to "get with the times". It actually sounds like it was all more funny than angry.) I tell her all about the tricks I'm trying to learn at the skatepark (switch flips are my current nemesis, where you put your non-dominant foot forward – it's like writing with your other hand, except you might fall over) and she tells me about fashion illustration, which she's only just got into but really loves. She's so good at it too. She wears cool outfits, and she imagines even cooler ones with asymmetric fits that look like they're from the future. She's good at everything. Weird that we don't run out of stuff to talk about when we talk all day Monday to Friday. Can you get closer than best friends? Is it just marriage after that? I mean marriage in, like, a friend way, obviously.

"So I'm thinking maybe I'll try to put together the most grandma-inappropriate outfit I can for next time we visit. Just to mess with Mum when I come downstairs; I'll change into something wholesome afterwards."

"What counts as grandma-inappropriate? Sudden noises? Racing?"

"Maybe for your grandma. Mine's a strong old girl."

"And yet she has to be protected from low necklines."

"Strong heart, old fashioned morals. I'd love to see what she'd make of a tattoo. Maybe I'll get some rub on ones."

"I can't believe you're willing to push your mum's buttons like that. I'm too scared to even get a trim."

She playfully ruffles my hair up.

"Careful, you'll ruin my 'do," I joke, pretending to preen.

"It's getting really long," she says.

I'm painfully aware. It's almost past my shoulders now. I try to imagine that I'm like a surfer guy, with windswept locks, but I know that's not at all how it looks.

"Yeah, I know. I am not a fan."

"You ever think maybe you could just cut it off, show up to school in your skateboarding clothes, tell Alex the truth and ask him to be your boyfriend and tell your mum you don't care if she doesn't like it?"

I laugh before I realize she isn't joking.

"Whoa. No, absolutely not. Is that what you'd do?"

She nods thoughtfully. "Probably, yeah."

"What's it like when *you* fight with your parents? Really fight, not 'let's give grandma a culture shock' fight." I'm curious. I think the way fights go in our house probably isn't the norm.

Mina thinks about it. "Well, they yell. I yell back." She laughs. "You're looking at me like I'm an alien."

"Nobody yells in my house. Mum panics, and me and Jamie try to calm her down."

"What do you mean, she panics?"

"Like, she cries a lot, and breathes really fast, and talks about all the bad things that have happened and all the worse things that could happen, and how scared she is, and then after that she's edgy and cold for days."

"But she doesn't get angry or shout at you?"

"Maybe it doesn't *sound* that bad, but ... it really scares me. I hate it."

"No, I get it, I can see how it could be really scary. That seems like a lot of pressure, for you to have to make *her* feel better when she gets upset like that."

"Yeah. And it seems like I bring it out so much worse than Jamie ever does. She seems to understand that he's his own person, whereas for me..."

"Well, she wants you to be like her, I guess."

"You're very wise."

"I know."

The bell rings and we start walking to class, enjoying the sun. Dani walks past, laughing with her friends about something. Mina glances at me nervously, like she thinks I might tackle Dani for stealing my man. Elena gives us a secret wave as the gang head inside.

"You're way better off without him, you know."

I wouldn't say that I want to be with Alex any more. The feelings aren't *gone*, but it's not exactly a crush now. Still, the rejection stings, and even inspired some brief attempts to wear mascara, which I'd really rather not talk about.

"Um … yeah, sure."

"OK, serious question, Jay."

"Shoot."

"Why did you like him?"

"That's a weird question. Why does anyone like anyone?"

"Did he make you laugh?"

"Um … *he* laughed at *my* jokes?"

"Mm, strike one. Did you really have proper conversations, *about* anything?"

"Once he told me about how his dad didn't support his skateboarding. That was a bonding moment."

"So you can think of one example."

"It doesn't sound good when you put it like that, but I swear we just vibed. Besides, I found him highly attractive."

"And tell me, what did you find attractive about him?"

"I mean, he's obviously incredibly good-looking, but that's not all of it. He's so good at skating, and his arms are so strong, and he dresses well and has good hair."

"I'd say at least a few of those sound like things you'd like to be yourself."

I blink. I hadn't thought about it like that… OK, SURE

there are some elements of his look that I would like to have myself but … it's definitely not the whole deal because I was attracted to him as well, but … why is Mina so perceptive?

"I'm going to need to do some more self-analysis about that one. But it's more than that. He saw the person I am." I wave sadly at my school skirt and hair. "No one else does."

Mina steps in front of me, stopping me short. I blink, surprised, and she stands there holding my gaze. She's so close that I can see every detail of her face, her wide brown eyes, her lashes. There's just enough lipgloss on her lips for the light to glint off them.

"*I do.*"

She half smiles, then walks away and into our classroom without looking back. I stare after her, feeling dizzy and confused.

I follow her into the classroom and slide into the seat next to her. She's looking at her books as she stacks them neatly on the desk, and she's smiling like she's trying not to laugh.

What is going on here?

I need Jamie's help. Even if it's just imaginary Jamie.

"Well, hellooooooo," Jamie says. He's wearing a toga like an ancient Greek god. He has wings, and he's holding a little bow and arrow.

"*The toga suits you, actually.*"

"*I know! I have the legs for it.*"

"I need your help."

"Of course. My advice in the ways of love."

"You saw what just happened, right? I need your assessment. Was that, or was that not A Moment?"

Jamie produces a bunch of chemistry equipment with brightly coloured liquids fizzing and popping. (I love that he always has props in these daydreams.) He sets them on a table and doesn't even look at them, just says:

"No."

"What?"

"Nope."

"You didn't even use your science stuff…"

"Didn't have to. That wasn't A Moment."

"Oh."

There's a pause. I look down at the ground.

"I KNEW IT!" Jamie yells, startling me.

"Ahh! What?"

"You're disappointed. You wanted *it to be A Moment!"*

"I did NOT!"

He draws a tiny arrow and aims it at me in his tiny bow.

"You like Mina!"

"I do not!" I duck behind his science things. *"She's my friend! That's all!"*

"Oh, yeah?" He keeps chasing me. *"How do you feel about Tom Proctor?"*

"I don't like him, and I wish he'd never talk to her again, but that's a coincidence!"

"That's jealousy, buddy."

"Don't shoot me with your tiny bow and arrow!"

"I'm afraid I'm a very good shot."

He fires his arrow and—

I jolt out of my daydream, just in time to get a question about tectonic plates completely wrong, which of course makes Mina tease me even more. My phone vibrates in my pocket and it's Mina. Her text says, "Stop staring angstily into the distance. You're missing out on the wonders of geography. What if you have to geograph in the future?"

I giggle so hard the teacher asks if something is funny.

At the end of the day, Mina grimly places a hand on my shoulder.

"Are you ready … for the penultimate Planning Committee meeting?"

"I don't think so."

I've avoided Dani more than usual since the Alex debacle. She seems to have got bored of mocking me and Mina anyway. Maybe the warmer weather has mellowed her. But I suspect she'll still be a nightmare in close quarters.

Mina takes a bag of sweets out of her pocket.

"Here, we can treat it like a drinking game. Have a sweet every time she says something hurtful."

I eye the bag. "Do you think there are enough in here?"

We walk slowly towards the meeting room as if we're walking to the gallows.

"Get inside, losers," Dani yells from the classroom. We walk in, taking a sweet each from the bag.

Dani gives us her usual appraising look (eyes quickly up and down from shoes to hair and back, judging everything on the way). All I can see when I look at her is her kissing Alex under the fairy lights on New Year's Eve. I sound bitter. I hope they're *very happy together*. OK, that sounds more bitter.

"We're picking a DJ and a photographer, and we really don't want your input," she says as we take our seats.

"Fantastic! We won't give it," I say.

Elena says hi very quietly, then leans over to me and whispers, "How's your brother?" with a shy little smile. They were flirting on New Year's and they've been crushing on each other ever since. Things still aren't quite right between me and Jamie, but he hasn't been able to stop himself bringing her up all the time.

"He's good."

"Wow," she says, smiling dreamily.

"Oh, look, Elena's talking about Jamie again," Dani says. "Hey, Jay, how does it feel to know your brother got all the looks?"

Mina passes me a sweet.

"Do you have siblings, Dani?" I ask, picturing her kissing Alex in the skatepark.

"No."

"So who got all the *empathy*?"

Mina snort–laughs. I'm pretty certain Dani is about to say something that will ruin my self-esteem and possibly my life, but Elena can't help leaning over to me again.

"Is he going to be waiting for you today, or—"

"Can you stop?" Dani snaps. "I am *so* bored of talking about Jamie, and how you kissed Jamie on New Year's, and how you're texting Jamie all the time."

Elena looks hurt.

Gertrude turns to Dani (I STILL haven't learned all of their real names). "Oh my god! How's it going with you and Alex?"

Dani gives a self-satisfied smile that makes me want to tackle her. "Really good. I'm just so glad that we're finally, like, officially a couple, you know?"

Fantastic. A dream come true. I've been hoping I'd get to hear Dani discuss the details of her and Alex's relationship.

"It was such a long time coming!!!" somebody gushes. I'm focusing everything I have on keeping my face as expressionless as possible.

"Yeah, I think we were both scared of commitment, and how much we liked each other," she says.

"Soooo, how far have you guys gone?" Mildred asks. I actually start to stand up to leave, but Mina catches me in her vice-like grip (how is she so strong?) and pins me to my chair before anybody notices. She catches my eye and very slightly shakes her head. She's right. I can't give anything away. There would be nothing worse than

212

Dani thinking that girl–Jay, the loser, has a crush on her boyfriend.

"I'll never tell," Dani says, teasingly. "But I will say … he's *such* a gentleman."

"Awwwww," the room choruses.

I start to join in with a sarcastic "aww" and Mina quickly shoves some sweets in my mouth. Then everybody starts talking about who to hire for the DJ and me and Mina are free to tune out.

"Are you OK?" she whispers.

"Oh, yeah, on top of the world, couldn't be happier for her," I whisper back.

"What is he *doing?* I don't think he likes her. I'm not sure he really likes girls."

"Maybe he just wants to be normal," I whisper, bitterly.

Mina swats me like a fly, making me jump. "Stop that," she says. "He's the most normal boy alive, Jay. The only unusual things about him are that he's good at brooding and doing flip kicks."

"They're called kickflips."

"Sure, that's what I said."

"I wish I could talk to him about it. Just to see if he's OK."

"You might be the last little Jesus superfan on earth he's ready to talk to about that."

"Never told him it was Jesus I was into. I just vaguely mentioned church."

"Which church?"

"My church. The church. It's in another town, you wouldn't know it."

"Which town?"

"The one … to the … West."

"Has Alex ever asked you one single question about yourself? Your story doesn't stand up to even, like, *slight* scrutiny."

"We mostly communicate through rail tricks and tortured silences. It's our thing."

"*Men*," Mina says, exasperated.

I hurry her out of the room as soon as the meeting ends, eager to get away from Dani. I feel sick and shaky, and it's not just because of all the sugar we ate.

"At least there's only one more Planning Committee left," Mina says. "Then we never have to see Dani again."

"Except for every day until we leave high school."

"Well, yes, but that's barely four years, right? It'll fly by."

"Hey, guys!"

We look round to see Ms George waving to us from inside her classroom.

"Hey, Ms George," Mina says, heading over to her, "you're staying late."

"Teachers usually do."

"You must get paid a lot," I say.

She laughs for a long time.

"We were at the Planning Committee meeting," Mina

says. "They were going to ask that guy from the boys' school who set a car on fire to be the DJ, but they're asking Elena's older brother instead, which I'm sure you'll be pleased to hear."

"That *is* good to know!" Ms George says. "It might have been OK if it was just the one car, but…"

"Oh," I say, "that's … not great."

"Well, he knows what he likes," she says drily. "I'm proud of you both for sticking it out with the Planning Committee. I think I owe you both an apology. Mina, you and Dani have been friends for so long I thought it was a shame not to try and patch things up. I thought you both being on the committee would help. But I am aware that has not worked."

"Yeah…" Mina says. "I mean, I guess I wouldn't say it's made things *worse,* at least?"

"Thanks," Ms George says, "but I really am sorry. I shouldn't have got involved."

It's a disconcerting experience, hearing an adult admit to being wrong. They don't often do that.

While me, Mum and Jamie sit at the dinner table having pasta that night, I think about when Mum said she'd try to be less "uptight" after New Year's Eve. She didn't actually *apologize,* did she? I don't think I've ever actually heard her say sorry to us. I know I say it to her all the time, though. Maybe I'm the one with things to apologize for. But surely she's in the wrong sometimes?

215

"Are you meeting Hugo this week?" she asks.

Even if she doesn't say sorry, she's trying to change for you. You should try to change for her. Or at least act like you are.

"Yeah!" I say. But it sounds half-hearted.

CHAPTER 18

I actually wish I liked Hugo, or that he was at least an actual therapist, because I feel like I could benefit from some therapy lately. There's so much on my mind. *Am I dressing like this for the right reasons? How can I resolve my complicated feelings around my complicated gay-ish kiss? Are my feelings for my best friend strictly bestfriendy?* But unfortunately I hate Hugo, which I'm painfully reminded of as I sit opposite him on Friday lunchtime. He's wearing his usual uniform of shorts, a polo shirt and a smug expression.

I promised Mum I'd try. And I have. I've been polite and more responsive. But I know it's still not really what she wants from me. I have that reckless feeling again – why don't I try giving her and Hugo *exactly* what they want?

I breeze into the meeting with my skirt rolled up the way Mina showed me and my hair pushed back out of my face for once.

"Sorry I'm late!" I say, crossing my legs the girl way (knee over knee, not ankle over knee). "I've been *so* busy with the Planning Committee."

He blinks. I don't know if he's going to buy this, but it's definitely going to be funny to find out.

"The Planning Committee?"

"Oh, have I not told you about it before? Me and the girls are working on planning the Summer Dance. It's so close now! Exciting."

I'm basically in character as Dani Hex at this point. Hugo is furiously taking notes.

"You're excited for the Summer Dance?"

"Totally! The theme we picked is *so cute*. Girls in pink and boys in blue. It's going to look great in the photographs."

He stares at me for a moment and I'm pretty sure I've gone too far. But then he breaks out in a smile.

"I have to say, Jennifer, it's great to see that you're getting on so well. You almost seem like a different person to who you were before Christmas."

"Oh, really?" I say, gritting my teeth. "What was I like?"

"You were so … negative and determined to alienate others. No offence, of course! Lots of teenagers have a phase where they're just desperate to be different, don't they?"

"Wow, yes, I think I have heard that," I say, looking at him with big eyes like he's said something interesting that I can't wait to hear more about. He actually looks proud.

"Yes, it's very common. But now you seem so much more positive, and you're obviously participating and fitting in with the girls. That's great!"

It occurs to me that maybe Hugo does know that I'm faking this, but he just doesn't care, because I'm faking the right thing. Either that or I'm a great actor. For the rest of the session I keep babbling about the dance, which he seems perfectly happy with. I'll have to wait to find out how he feeds back to Mum. There is a chance he'll tell her I've simply snapped.

But if I'm honest with myself, I know they'll both prefer this fake version of Jennifer.

After lunch, in physics with Mr Norwood, our sleepiest and least observant teacher, me and Mina debrief yet again about Alex and Dani's blossoming relationship.

"I think he's a pushover," Mina says, rolling her eyes. "It sounds like he's just gone along with what Dani wants and can't tell her he doesn't like her, or tell *you* what he's got himself into. You might as well get a nice houseplant and stick a fringe on it, it would be the same."

"I still feel bad for that poor, beautiful houseplant. He's too scared to stand up for himself."

"So much for the cliché of men being assertive and confident and unafraid of confrontation."

"Maybe I'm a better boy than him," I say brightly.

"Well, let's not get ahead of ourselves, you're so afraid of confrontation that you have two lives."

OK, she has a point. But it's not because I'm scared.

Well, maybe it is because I'm scared.

"In this day and age, Mina, boys can be whatever they want. They can be cowards if that's what they want to be."

"Mm. So why can't a girl have short hair?"

"Leave me alone. Anyway, can we talk about you for once? We're always talking about me and my crush."

"Wow, Jay, you're becoming self-aware!"

We spend a few minutes throwing pencils at each other (Mr Norwood has really got to start paying attention) before I say, "So what about you and your crush?"

"Me and my crush? Who's that?"

She's looking straight at me and it makes me feel nervous for some reason.

"Tom Proctor?"

She laughs.

"And why do you think I have a crush on Tom Proctor?"

I have a little moustache and I've gathered Mina and Tom Proctor in the drawing room.

"I suppose you're wondering why I've gathered you all here," I say.

"Is it still gathering when there's only two people?" Mina asks.

"Thanks for inviting me!" Tom says cheerily.

"Quiet, both of you!" I say. *"I present my evidence. Mina and Tom, on December thirty-first did you not flirt at Elena's party? On January twenty-first, did you, Tom, not buy Mina her favourite chocolate bar after school and did you, Mina, not return the favour on February third by offering to share a bag of sweets with Mr Proctor? On March twentieth did Tom not hear you saying you hadn't been bowling for ages and say, 'Oh, hey, maybe we should go together sometime,' and did you not say, 'Oooh, yeah, maybe!'? I accuse you ... of a CRUSH!"*

It's probably better not to admit I've been watching them quite that closely.

"You guys were pretty flirty at Elena's party, right?"

"You think *that's* who I was flirting with?"

There's a pause and she doesn't break eye contact. I can feel my heart rate speeding up and my adrenaline rising. Why does talking to her lately feel like that thing in skating where you're so scared to go down a ramp or try a trick that you just stand there, like a deer in the headlights on a skateboard? For a second I imagine a more confident version of myself.

I am six feet tall and all rippling muscle. I barely fit behind my desk. My hair is upsettingly perfect, my teeth uncomfortably white.

"Well, obviously I think you were flirting with me."

"Somebody's arrogant."

"Arrogant? Or just the man of your dreams?"

I lean down to kiss her as epic music starts to play...

OK, where did that come from?!

"Uh, yeah. No? Maybe. I don't know."

Great. Very suave.

My phone buzzes. It's Alex. I freeze, suddenly not wanting Mina to see that he's messaged me. I almost don't care what the message says, which is so different from how I would have felt even a month ago. Of course, curiosity gets the better of me.

"I'm really sorry about everything."

Just that. It's nice. I glance over at Mina, taking notes in her neat handwriting, and suddenly it feels crystal clear that I just want to be Alex's friend. I reply.

"Thanks. It's all right. Let's talk next time I see you."

Ms George catches me at the end of the day, a green shawl draped around her shoulders and her hair bouncing faster than usual as she hurries down the hallway. Even though she's in a rush she breaks out smiling when she waves at me.

"I'm afraid I can't make our usual catch up next

222

Monday, but I just wanted to check how your meeting with Hugo was?"

"It was OK for once. I just talked about the Planning Committee; he loved it."

She looks confused.

"Why?"

"Something about me participating and fitting in with the other girls or whatever, I don't really remember. But the most important thing is that my mum will be happy when he tells her."

"He tells your mum what you talk about?"

"Yeah, why?"

"He's not a counsellor so there's no reason why he shouldn't, technically, but it doesn't seem like that gives you much space to relax and open up."

"Oh, don't worry! I wouldn't open up to Hugo. I only go to those meetings so that Mum knows I'm still trying to change." I catch myself by surprise with how straightforward I've been. That *is* the only reason I put up with him.

Ms George looks sad and carefully sets a hand on my shoulder. "Jay, she shouldn't want to change you."

"I have to go," I say quickly, walking away. I don't want to think about what she's saying. I don't want her to be right.

Jamie hasn't waited for me – he's stopped doing that. As soon as I open the door I can tell Hugo has spoken to Mum, because she's standing there beaming, freshly dyed blonde hair and sparkly silver blouse glinting in the afternoon sunlight. She's practically a traffic hazard.

"I didn't know you were so excited about the Summer Dance! Pink and Blue is such a nice idea for a theme. Tomorrow, why don't I take you and Mina dress shopping?"

"Yeah!" I say, slipping past her into the hallway and towards my room, trying to sound enthusiastic. "That sounds great!"

"Jamie!" she calls.

He leans out of his bedroom door. "Yeah?"

"I'm taking Jennifer and Mina dress shopping tomorrow for the Summer Dance, why don't you come along and look at suits?"

Even though we've got distant I can see sympathy in his eyes when he sees my expression.

"Bit early, isn't it?" he asks. "The Summer Dance isn't until ... you know, summer."

"We don't have to buy anything yet, it's just nice to get an idea of what you like, and see what's out there."

There's no way we can get out of it. Mum looks delighted with her plan. We both nod and share a grim look as we head into our rooms to spend the evening alone.

I call Mina as soon as my door is shut.

"Miss me already?" she says, picking up straight away.

"Obviously. I've been a wreck since you left me. What are you doing tomorrow?"

"Not a thing."

"Then I have fantastic news. My mother wants to take us dress shopping."

"Oh dear."

"Yep."

CHAPTER 19

I look terrible.

I mean, I've looked terrible ever since we moved here. Some days it bothers me more than others. Today it bothers me a lot.

I'm standing in a cubicle in a changing room, staring at my reflection in a hot pink dress with frilly sleeves. Someone please tell me: what does a frilled sleeve contribute to the world? What does it do? It certainly doesn't look good. Or at least it doesn't look good on *me*.

"Come out and show us!" Mum calls from outside the door. For a second I seriously consider refusing. Maybe I could crawl out under the dividing wall into the next cubicle, and then the next, and the next, and sprint out of the shop. But that's not going to happen. All I can really hope for is that she doesn't make me buy it.

I open the door. Mum and Mina are standing there waiting for me, and Jamie is on a bench behind them, wearing a blue suit and looking bored. He puts his hand over his mouth when he sees me and just barely manages to stifle the laugh. I look like a birthday cake.

"Well, that's gorgeous!" Mum exclaims. I think Mina is only managing not to laugh because she can tell I'm upset. I can't even look her in the eye. Her seeing me looking like this is horrible. It's bad enough that she sees me in that awful school skirt every day, and this is a whole other level.

"What do you think, Mina?" Mum asks.

"Um..." Mina looks me up and down, then says, "It's obviously ... really nice, but maybe it's a little bit elaborate for Jay...nnifer. I think Jennifer might suit something a bit more simple and elegant, you know?"

"Oooh, interesting!" says Mum, clearly wishing once again that Mina was her daughter. "We'll have to look at some more options. Mina, you should try on the dress you picked out."

"I will!" Mina slips into the changing room next door to me and I step back into mine.

"I'm just going to take this off for now," I say loudly to Mum. "It's just so ... delicate and pretty, I'm scared I'll hurt

227

it!" I finish with a slightly hysterical laugh and hear Mina snort in her cubicle.

I come back out wearing the too-tight jeans and T-shirt that Mum deemed feminine enough to buy me ("though you really should wear skirts more often, Jennifer, you have such lovely legs!") and sit next to Jamie.

He leans over to whisper to me, "You looked like a birth—"

"Birthday cake, yes, I know."

He giggles. "Ah, I'm sorry. Hopefully she won't make you buy it."

"We can only pray."

Mina swings the cubicle door open and steps out. "What do you think?"

My mind goes absolutely blank for several seconds. Mina looks *incredible*. She's wearing a blush pink dress that ends above the knees. The top half is tight with no sleeves and the skirt is a little bit looser, so it swishes around a little bit when she moves.

"Oh! Sweetheart, you look beautiful," Mum says.

"Yeah, you look great!" Jamie says.

Mina looks at me. I feel Jamie looking at both of us, from one to the other.

"You should buy that," I say quietly. She raises one eyebrow, smiles, and swishes back into the changing room.

She does buy the dress, and luckily I convince Mum that although the birthday cake is stunning, I need more time to choose. Jamie buys the powder-blue suit he tried on, after promising Mum that he won't have another growth spurt before the dance. Me, Mum and Jamie say goodbye to Mina outside the shop.

"See you on Monday," she says, leaning in to give me a quick hug. "Shame I can't wear this."

"Shame you can't wear it all the time," I agree.

"Listen…" she says, quietly enough that only I can hear, "you should talk to your mum. No one should be forced to wear stuff they hate. OK?"

She walks off down the street.

I turn around to find Jamie watching me. "What?" he says.

"What?"

"You were staring."

"Was I? I don't think I was."

"You know in cartoons, where someone's eyes turn into hearts and pop out of their head…"

I roll my eyes and give him a shove as we head home. It almost feels like normal times.

I'm lying in my room doodling stickmen doing backside tail slides (I STILL can't do them) when there's a gentle knock on the door.

"Come in!" I say, sliding the notebook under my pillow.

Jamie comes in with his shopping bag.

"Thought you might want to try on my suit," he says.

My stomach hurts with how much I want us to be friends again. *Of course* I want to try on his suit.

"You know me too well," I say, sliding it out of the bag.

"I'm sorry stuff has been so weird with us," he says, turning away to let me change.

"Don't be," I say. "It's my fault."

"Still, I just wanted to say that I get it, and I know why you felt like you had to hide it, but I know, and it's OK."

I know, and it's OK. What does Jamie think he knows? I keep ending up in confusing but ultimately humorous conversations where I think people are talking about one thing but they're actually talking about another thing, and I'm getting good at spotting them. There's no way he knows about Alex. So what *is* he talking about?

"Oh yeah?" I say vaguely, buttoning up Jamie's white shirt. "You know, huh?"

"Yeah. It's obvious, really."

"Is it?"

"Completely. I can't believe Mum didn't notice."

"Good thing she hasn't!" Whatever it is.

"It's obvious, the way you look at her."

The way I look at Mum?

"And the way she looks at you."

The way Mum looks at me?

"It's so clear that you're together."

NOT MUM. *Mina.* No, that's ridiculous. I'm about to tell him so – but then I stop. A secret relationship with

Mina would explain everything: why I've been so distant with Jamie, and why I've been lying to him. I won't have to tell him about Alex. All I want is for Jamie to forgive me, and he looks so happy right now, and I'm on the spot...

So I smile bashfully and put my hands up like I've been caught out. "Has anyone ever told you that you're too perceptive?"

"It has been said."

"I'm so sorry I lied to you about it, Jamie. I was just scared about people knowing."

"Hey!" he says as I slide on the jacket. "You look great!"

I turn to the mirror. I *do* look great.

"I *love* it!" I gasp, reaching up to pull my hair back. "Why don't we wear these all the time?"

"Maybe we should. Maybe *you* should. To the Summer Dance, at least."

Staring at myself in the mirror, it feels possible. For a second.

"Imagine how much Mum would flip."

"So let her flip. Her making you try that dress on today when it was obvious how much you hated it was just ... horrible." Both him and Mina have said it now. Even Ms George has kind of said it. Maybe it isn't OK that she wants me to wear stuff I don't even like. Especially given how good this suit looks on me. It's slightly too big in the shoulders, but otherwise it's perfect.

"Anyway, why were you so scared to tell me about Mina? I've always thought you probably liked girls."

"Yes, I know. You've brought it up pretty much weekly since we were seven. I think I was scared to tell anyone about it … because I like her so much," I say.

Jamie nods, punches me on the arm, and it seems like everything is forgiven. I feel bad for lying to him. Again.

Because I definitely don't like Mina. Not that way. Definitely not.

Maybe it sounds like I'm in denial but I'm not; I'm just being clear about the fact that that's not how I feel, OK?

Good.

CHAPTER 20

So even though me and Jamie aren't technically twins, our birthdays are really close together, which means joint birthday parties. I like that because it takes the pressure off mine and I don't like my birthday that much, because teachers always tell everyone about it and then they all have to awkwardly say happy birthday to you. Also, I receive a stack of gifts that I will never use from Mum and other distant relatives. I have *so much* eyeshadow that I don't know what I'm supposed to do with. I mean, I do know I'm supposed to shadow my eyes with it, but I'd rather not. Whenever I've tried, the look is "flirtatious raccoon".

At breakfast on Sunday, while me and Jamie are working through bowls of cereal, Mum brings up the annual birthday party.

"So the big day's only a few weeks off! What do the birthday boy and birthday girl feel like doing?" she asks. "You can invite as many people here as you want!"

Jamie and I glance at each other. The thing is, Mum has always insisted on being at our birthday party, and she's not what I would call a relaxed parent. These birthday parties aren't exactly *fun*. It's less a question of how many to invite and more "which of our friends like us enough to forgive us for inflicting it on them".

Me and Jamie meet to conference in the garden and slump down on the lawn to decide who to curse with an invite to the party. This year our birthdays are in the break just before Summer term starts, so maybe everyone will be away on holiday and we won't have to worry about it.

"So obviously Mina," he says.

"Don't say that we're together, by the way!" I babble. "We're not ready to tell people yet, you know?"

"Of course!"

I breathe a sigh of relief. At least Jamie won't mention to Mina that she's my girlfriend, because she a) doesn't know I've told him and b) isn't. Why does lying create so many problems when it's so useful in the moment? "I'll bring the Toms."

"Oh, yeah. Tom Proctor."

Jamie laughs, leaning back on the grass.

"Yes, he fancies your girlfriend, but try to ignore that. And it's not his fault he's built like a Greek God."

"Yeah, does he *have* to be shaped like that?"

"He can't help it. Moving on."

"I only really want Mina to come. Maybe Elena."

"Actually, I'd also like to invite Elena."

"Oooooooooh!"

"Shh."

"Are you guys official yet?"

"No … but on New Year's we kissed at midnight. It was really cute."

"Adorable."

"We've been texting since then. We've gone on a few, like, coffee dates."

"Coffee dates! You sound like an adult in a rom-com. In New York."

"Thanks, I'm very mature. I was thinking I would maybe ask her to be my girlfriend soon."

"That's exciting. A huge commitment."

"Right? We better pick out a school for the kids soon. Maybe we'll even kiss again at some point."

"Yeah." I pull a strand of grass out of the ground and tear it up, thinking about the one kiss I've ever had. "It's much harder to kiss someone when it *isn't* New Year's Eve."

"Exactly, it just feels like there's less of a reason to do it."

"JENNIFER."

Jamie and I both flinch and look at each other in alarm. It's Mum, and she's upset. But what could have gone wrong? A few minutes ago she was in such a good mood...

She storms out of the house, holding my phone. We spring up. My mind races through what she could have seen. In my panicked state I honestly couldn't say I haven't been using that phone for crimes. What crimes? I don't know, but I must have done something.

"Who is Alex?"

Oh, no. *Oh, no.*

"Alex is a friend... Why are you looking at my phone?"

"'I wanted to kiss you for a really long time,'" she reads aloud.

"*What?*" Jamie says.

"That's just ... a joke..." I stammer. I feel like I'm underwater. "Why are you reading my texts?"

"Don't play with me, Jennifer."

"*Alex?*" Jamie whispers furiously.

"You need to text this girl right now, and tell her that you won't be seeing her again."

Without thinking, I say, "Alex is a boy."

Mum looks genuinely taken aback. She blinks. "A boy?"

God, is there NO ONE who even thinks I MIGHT be straight?

All three of us are looking from one to another, like

we're waiting to see who will shoot first. How high is the garden fence? Can I jump over it?

Mum turns to Jamie. "He must go to your school, Jamie. Do you know him?"

"Oh, yes, I know him," Jamie says, staring me down as I try to use my eyebrows to tell him to stop. "Jennifer's boyfriend, Alex. Why don't you explain that text? A lover's tiff, perhaps?"

Oh god. He's out for blood.

"Boyfriend?" Mum says, but she doesn't sound upset. She actually sounds pretty pleased. "Why didn't you tell me about him?"

For the second time in two days, I put myself in a fake relationship. I'm absolutely swamped with imaginary partners. "We've only just got together. It's been complicated."

"I'll say!" Jamie says with a hysterical chuckle.

"Well." Mum gathers herself and gives me a smile. "I see. I, ah, overreacted." *That's* the problem? *Not that she read my private messages?* "You should invite him to the party, Jennifer."

"What a great idea," Jamie says. "In fact, I'll text him right now."

He takes out his phone and starts typing. I shake my head at him furiously, but I can see his only goal now is chaos.

"I'm excited to meet him," Mum says.

"I'm *also* excited for you to meet him," Jamie says.

Mum stands there awkwardly for another second, then sets my phone down (on the ground, for some reason, like it might explode) and glides back into the house like nothing has happened.

A strange feeling grows in my stomach as I stare at the phone. At first I think I'm just sick from the adrenaline, because, *oh boy*, I feel like I've been skydiving. But it's not that.

It's that I don't respect Mum any more.

She doesn't care about me being happy. She cares about me being *normal*, whatever it might cost me. So what if Alex was a girl? I can't change it if I like girls. I thought maybe I could change the way I look and eventually get used to it. But maybe I can't change that, either.

I run a hand through my long hair. Why am I doing this? Why am I doing any of this? And for the first time, I think about – *really think* about – the reason we moved. What happened was bad, and scary, but was it really my fault?

Or did Mum just tell me it was?

"Ow!"

While I've been having an important moment of self-reflection and growth, Jamie has collected a handful of pebbles and is pelting me with them one by one. He pelts me again.

"*Jamie!*"

"Don't 'Jamie' me!"

"It's your name!"

"*Alex? How?*"

"We're casual skatepark acquaintances! And we kissed one time!"

"What do you think 'acquaintance' means?! When did you kiss?"

I dodge another pebble, which clatters against the fence. "On New Year's Eve; nothing else has happened!"

"I thought he was dating Dani Hex."

"He is now. Though he did say he was gay, then."

"*Alex is gay?*"

"Why are you and Mina both so surprised by that? Did you expect him to wear feather boas or something?"

Jamie flaps his hands. "Mina! What about Mina? You finally settle down with a nice girl and you immediately cheat on her with a boy who is all cheekbone and no wit! What are you doing?!"

"OK, Jamie, I may have told you several lies…"

He pelts me. *Ouch ouch ouch.*

"Unbelievable. You're unbelievable."

"Nothing is happening with me and Mina."

"But the chemistry! It was undeniable! Tell me everything. Now."

"I will. For real, this time." I sit down on the ground and start to speak in a hushed voice. "So the simple version is, I had a crush on Alex and then on New Year's I saw him kissing Dani Hex and then I went to the skatepark in my boys' clothes and I saw him there and I yelled at him about it and then we kissed. And Mina saw. And after that Alex stopped talking to me, but I was trying to talk to him to tell him who I really was but then he started going out with Dani Hex without telling me but then I saw them together and then we didn't talk for ages until he texted me the other day apologizing. And that brings us right up to now. Except … well, maybe you're a tiny bit right about Mina. Maybe there *is* chemistry. I'm not sure."

"That's not simple! Those are not simple events!"

"I'm as confused as you are! And I think I've made a lot of mistakes this year, and I think the worst one is messing up our friendship. Or our siblingship, or whatever you want to call it. But I've told you everything now, I promise, and I'm really, really sorry. I wanted to tell you the whole time, but everything just got out of hand, and I think I started to find it hard to tell you the truth. It feels like you always tell me to be honest and be myself, but everyone likes who you are. Even my own mother is just desperate to give me a makeover."

He thoughtfully pelts me with his last few pebbles. I accept it stoically.

"You should have told me. I'll never understand if you don't tell me."

"You're right. It's no excuse, but it's been kind of a weird year."

"I do get it. I hadn't realized you'd feel like that, but after last year, it really makes sense."

"Thank you. And I'm really sorry. Are we … OK? Do you want more pebbles?"

"Are you done with the lies?"

"I am. I think I am."

"Then we're OK. And I'm sorry I just invited Alex to our birthday party."

"Oh god. Has he replied?"

"Not yet."

"Why do you even have his number?"

"I got notes off him for a class last term. They weren't very good. Guess he was too busy questioning his sexuality. It sounds like just avoiding him might be for the best, you know?"

"No, I still want to tell him the truth. I told him we could talk next time we saw each other."

"Hm. I'm not sure you should stop lying to *every*one, maybe keep one or two of them going. Who knows how he'll react; I don't want you to get hurt."

I smile. "Thanks for looking out for me. But I want to do this. In fact, there's quite a lot of things I want to do. I've let Mum tell me what to do ever since what happened last year, and it's time to stop."

Jamie grabs me in a hug. "There's my brave little guy! I'll be right there with you."

"Oh my god, I didn't tell you! I can do hardflips now!"

"You can do hardflips?!"

And just like that, it's all back to normal. Guess he might have had a point about being honest/being myself/ not constructing an elaborate web of lies.

I missed my brother.

CHAPTER 21

For the last week of Spring term, I don't see Alex at the skatepark. I'd sort of hoped he'd come by so we could talk, but it's fair enough if he needs time, I guess. Plus, skating alone gives me more time to think.

Most of the time, I think about Mina.

Or rather, I try not to think about her and I fail.

I think Jamie might be (as usual) right. I definitely feel … something for Mina. A large and concerning something.

The thing is, Mina is the best friend I've ever had. If I like her, and she doesn't like me, then that's ruined. I don't want to lose her.

As we walk to school together on Friday, Jamie tries yet again to convince me to ask Mina out.

"She's so funny."

"Yes."

"She's incredibly good-looking."

"I'm aware."

"Remember the pink dress?"

"Yes, I remember the dress; I will probably never forget the dress."

"You'll 'never forget it'? And you're still not sure if you like her or not?"

"Feelings are confusing, Jamie."

"Across every gender, where you're concerned."

"Please tell me Alex still hasn't replied."

"Still nothing. He hasn't said anything in class, either. Which is kind of embarrassing for me, actually, isn't it? I invite the dude to my birthday and he gives me *nothing*."

We walk in silence for a moment.

"Just imagine how much better off you'd be with Mina…"

"Yes, Jamie, I agree, thank you."

At school, I feel like I can't be normal around Mina, no matter how hard I try. We're packing up our things after history and I'm attempting to tell her the story of Mum reading my texts from Alex, because I know she'll find it funny. "So she was all set to ban me from ever seeing imaginary girl Alex again, and as soon as she found out he was a boy she was just like, 'Oh, cool, you have a boyfriend, great, bring him over'."

"Your mum thinks you're going out with Alex? Let's hope she never speaks to Dani Hex."

"Yeah, it really wasn't my finest hour. I just panicked because she seemed so angry about imaginary girl Alex."

"Poor imaginary girl Alex. She must be heartbroken."

"Ha, yeah. I mean, I probably wouldn't date an imaginary girl, of course. Or maybe I would. I don't know."

"I wouldn't have a crisis over it; she's imaginary."

"You're right. I'll save my crises for real girls." I turn bright red, as I remember that Mina is a real girl who I'm having a real crisis over. "That's a joke. I'm joking."

"You seem incredibly tense."

"Leftover adrenaline from finally telling Jamie the truth, maybe."

"Mm. I'd love to hear all the secrets you tell him."

"Oh, no, you wouldn't. They're all boring and not about anyone we know. It's mostly skincare. And shortcuts." Thankfully someone bumps into me on their way out of class, providing a brief distraction from all of the things I just said.

"I got you a birthday present, by the way. But I don't want to give it to you in front of your mum. Do you want to come stay at mine after your party?"

"Sure, that would be cool … friend."

"Friend? Did you just call me friend, like, as a proper noun?"

"You're the smart one, Mina, you tell me whether things are proper nouns or not. Look at that! Time for my lunchtime session. I have to go."

I scramble and leave, ignoring Mina's giggling as I drop a pencil, fail to pick it up, and eventually abandon it. But I don't go to meet Hugo. Instead, I go to Ms George's classroom, where she eats lunch. It's time to start making changes.

"Hi, Jay," she says, waving at me with her book.

It's time to stand up for myself. For what I believe in. To confront my demons.

"Ms George, I don't want to talk to Hugo. Can you tell him I'm quitting?"

I was expecting some sort of discussion about it, but she just gives me a salute, puts her book down, and walks out of the door, saying, "Say no more. Stay there."

I wait for about ten minutes. I wonder if she's fighting him. There's just something about Ms George that seems like she knows how to fight. Hugo is probably a bit taller, but Ms George is pretty solidly built, and I've seen her pick up a desk to move it like it's nothing. If she got close enough to grab him, I think it would be over.

Ms George vaults over the ropes and into the ring. Hugo jabs and swings with his long arms, but she's too quick. With lightning speed, she darts in close and grabs him around the waist. The crowd scream as she hoists him into the air and hurls him full-force into the ground, slamming him down on to his back. The referee throws himself between them before she can finish Hugo off with a body slam. The bell rings and the referee grabs her wrist, thrusting her arm into the air as the crowd chants her name.

"Ms George! Ms George! Ms George…"

Sure, it's not the greatest wrestling name, but that doesn't matter when you're a champion…

"Done," Ms George says, sweeping back into the classroom, adjusting her hoop earrings.

Wow. Maybe she did take him out.

"Thanks," I say, "that was really quick."

"And fun! For me," she says with a smug smile. "So why the sudden change?"

"I've been twisting myself up like a pretzel for so long, trying to make other people happy with who I am … or trying to be someone else, who would be safe, and not thinking enough about who I want to be. I just got too twisted up. Every pretzel has a breaking point, I guess." It's nice to start saying this stuff out loud. I can't believe it's taken me so long to put it all into words.

Ms George considers me for a long moment and very kindly doesn't mention that pretzels don't tend to crack under pressure. Not the soft ones, anyway.

"Sounds like some big changes are coming."

"Yeah, I hope so."

CHAPTER 22

The day of the birthday party I wake up and put on my least offensive girl-clothes, but I pack the clothes Jamie gave me at the start of the year into a backpack. I stay quiet through breakfast and try to ignore how excited Mum is about possibly meeting my nice straight boyfriend.

"Would he like to arrive a little early to have some lunch with us?"

"Uh, like I said, I don't think he can make it."

"Your boyfriend has to come to your birthday party!"

"Well, it was kind of short notice, and he's had a family thing scheduled for months."

"That's nice, that he's family oriented."

"Uh–huh."

Me and Jamie help set up a table of snacks, whispering to each other as the radio plays.

"Still nothing from Alex, right?"

"Nope. I think we're safe."

"OK, great. Are you excited to see Elena?" I ask, wiggling my eyebrows.

"Shut up. Are you excited to see Mina?"

"Shut up."

"Jennifer," Mum says, bustling in with a bowl of dip, "are you sure you wouldn't rather wear the dress I bought you for your birthday?"

I knew The Dress would keep coming up today. It's actually pretty nice. You know, for someone else. It's green, and Mum said it's called a skater dress, which is ironic. But I am never going to wear it. I'm not even going to try it on.

"I told you, Mum, we're all going to go to the park after this because the weather is so nice. I don't want to get it dirty."

"That's a good point," she says. "The fabric is so pretty, isn't it?"

"Yeah, very … handsome."

"Still, though, it's always nice for a girl to be the centre of attention on her birthday, isn't it? I remember my fifteenth birthday. All of my girl friends threw me a surprise party. They'd even clubbed together to pay someone to come do my hair and make-up. I felt so beautiful. Cassie organized it – you remember Cassie."

I do remember Mum's friend Cassie. I see her about once a year when Mum has her own parties. She's very nice, but she has a tendency to hold me by the face when she talks to me.

"It's not every day you get to be the belle of the ball," Mum says wistfully.

I feel like I'm starting to understand Mum better. She loves being "a girl", and she wants me to have everything that she had. But it's not me. Why doesn't she care that it's not me?

"There are four people coming, Mum."

"I do wish you two would make larger friendship circles," Mum says, sighing. Jamie gives me the faintest eye roll. A bunch more people are going to be at the park later, where she can't bother them. Mostly Jamie's friends, admittedly.

Mina arrives first, looking adorable in black jeans and a white T-shirt that's sort of flowy. There's a little bit of pink around her eyes, but it's really subtle. I love looking at what she's wearing. I'm so hyper aware of it, I feel like I'm compiling a police report every time I look at her.

A police officer lets himself into the interrogation room and sits down opposite me. My lawyer beside me gives me a nod. It's time to talk.

"What kind of shoes was the suspect wearing?"

"Those flat white trainers for playing tennis, with like a little pink logo on the side that kind of matches her eyeshadow, but it's really subtle so you wouldn't say it was overly matchy matchy."

"Would you say the overall look was simple but extremely cute?"

"That's exactly what I'd say, officer."

"Would you go on to say that you have an enormous crush on the suspect?"

"Shut up, officer."

"May I remind you that you're under oath?"

"That's only in court. We're not in court. You're mixing up your daydream locations."

"Happy birthdays!!!" Mina shrieks, grabbing me and Jamie around the necks in a double hug.

"Thank you!"

"Sixteen and fifteen. Ripe old ages. Jay, did your mum say you can stay at mine tonight?"

Jamie starts an eyebrow wiggle and I quietly stamp on his foot.

"Yep! We're all good. We're gonna hang out here for a few hours, then we'll go to the park and then I'll grab my stuff from here on the way to yours."

"A beautiful plan. Talk me through this snack table. Where should I start?"

"I'd start over here at the savoury end, with the chips and dips, and work up to the biscuits and chocolate buttons."

The Toms are the next to arrive. Tom Proctor grins when he sees Mina and offers to get her a drink like they're in a bar, or something. He awkwardly pours her a plastic cup of Diet Coke.

"As if you couldn't get your own drink," I mutter while he's talking to Jamie.

"Nice of someone to offer though, isn't it?" she says, smirking.

"Oh. Oh – would you … like a drink?"

"No, thanks, I've got one." She grins, patting me on the cheek like a puppy. I'm trying to think of something (anything) to say back when Little Tom bounces over.

"Hi, Jay! Happy birthday," he beams, little round glasses glinting.

"Thanks, Tom! Glad you could come. Can I get you a drink?"

"Sure!"

"Oh, so Little Tom gets a drink?" Mina whispers as I pour him one.

"Try not to be too jealous."

The doorbell rings. Jamie rushes over to open it.

"Elena!"

"Hi, Jamie," she says, looking shiny and excited.

"Can I get you a drink?" he asks.

Mina giggles next to me.

"OK, I get it now," I say. "I should have offered you a drink. The second your glass is empty I'm going to offer you one. You won't even have time to be thirsty, that's how fast I'm going to be."

"Wow, the service at this party is really good."

With a flash of confidence that I think surprises both of us, I offer her a tray of strawberries and say, "And your waiter's hot."

She laughs and shoves me as Elena comes over to say hello.

"Hi, Mina, hi, Jay," she says. "Sorry I'm late. I was waiting outside so that I wouldn't look too keen, because I really fancy your brother. But don't tell him. Or maybe do? I don't know, actually. Maybe I should tell your brother that I fancy your brother."

I really like Elena. She's so sweet, even if she does hang out with Dani. I love how she talks like she's taken a low dose of truth serum or something. Jamie keeps glancing over at her, which is cute. I think they'd be good together.

Mum is doing the rounds and introducing herself to everybody when the doorbell rings again. I look around, confused. Everyone is already here, no one else was invited. Unless … *oh no*. I look round and meet Jamie's eyes. He's staring at me, panicked.

"I'll get it," he says, about an octave higher than usual.

"Mina. Can you hide me?" I whisper urgently.

"No offence, Jay, but this isn't the best attended birthday party I've ever seen. I think you'd be missed."

"No, Mina, seriously, I think that might be—"

"Alex!" Jamie squeaks, "You … are here!"

Mina immediately lunges in front of me.

"Uh, yeah," Alex says, "you told me to come, right? And you said the Toms would be here?"

"I did say that. It's true. They are here. You just didn't reply to my text."

"Oh. Yeah, sorry. Should I … go?"

Despite being over that crush, I feel my heart melt a little bit. He's so *vulnerable*. I bet no one invites him to things because they think he doesn't want to come, but he actually really does and he's just shy. How adorable is that? Sometimes beautiful people have problems too.

"No. Don't go. Come in. Toms, look. It's Alex."

The Toms say hello. Me and Jamie both have our eyes fixed on Mum as she breaks out into a huge smile and takes a step towards Alex. I feel like I'm watching a train crash in slow motion.

"Alex," she says, "you came! I'm so glad to meet you."

"Uh, you too."

"Jennifer will be so…"

There's a crash. Everybody looks round to see Jamie standing over a shattered plate, crisps everywhere.

"Oh no," he says. "I can be so clumsy."

"I'll clean that up," Mum says, hurrying into the kitchen.

Nice one, Jamie. But there are only so many plates he can break.

"Hey, Mina," Alex says, "Elena."

"Hey," they both say. Mina stays firmly planted in front of me. There's a long pause while everyone stands in silence, and I realize with a jolt that Alex is waiting for someone to introduce him to the only person in the room he doesn't know. Jamie seems to realize it at the same time.

"That's my sister," he blurts. "Jay-nniffer. Jennifer."

"Cool. Hi," Alex says, and turns away to talk to the Toms. He barely even glances at me. Wow. And phew. Mum finishes sweeping up the crisps and fixes her gaze back on Alex. I'm frozen, like in one of those dreams where you can't run.

"So, Alex," she says, interrupting his conversation with the Toms, "how did you meet—"

"Alex!" Mina says, too loudly. Everyone turns around and looks at her.

"Yes?" he says, after a long pause.

"Have you, um, been here before?" she says desperately.

"No."

"Then Jamie better give you … the tour?"

"Yes!" Jamie yelps. "The tour! Come on!" He grabs Alex by the arm and drags him out of the room.

"We've never had a tour," Little Tom says.

"Then you better go too," Mina says. "And you, Elena. I've had the tour before. And Jay-nnifer, of course, lives here, so she's had it too. We'll stay here. Have fun!"

"Let's go, tour!" Jamie says, leading the group into the hallway.

Mum looks baffled. She shakes her head. "Those boys," she says.

"Hide me, Mina," I hiss. "There aren't a lot of rooms in this house, we don't have long."

"I don't think I've ever experienced this much adrenaline," she whispers. "How have you been leading this double life for *months*?"

"I don't know, I'm literally scared all the time."

Mum joins us, still beaming. "Well, Alex seems very polite. And he's so handsome!"

"Yeah, that's Alex. A real … man's man," Mina jabbers. Maybe it's her we need to hide.

"And over here we have the kitchen…" I hear Jamie saying. All of us are clearly at breaking point. Nobody is functioning properly. "Isn't it such a lovely day?" he's asking hysterically as he leads his confused group of tourists back into the living room.

"It *is* a lovely day," I say, putting on a strange, high-pitched voice in the hopes that Alex won't recognize me (and also because I'm panicking). "Why don't we all go to the park right now?"

"But we haven't cut the cake yet," says Mum.

"We'll come back later!" Jamie says. "It would be a terrible shame to miss the … light."

Mum is looking at me suspiciously. Then she smiles and

says in a stage whisper, "Of course, you've never introduced me to a boyfriend before. You're so shy!"

"You have a boyfriend?" Elena asks, looking at the Toms.

The boys overhear her and look over with interest. Alex looks at the Toms. The Toms look at Alex. The Toms look at each other. Any of them could theoretically be my boyfriend, though they all know it's not them.

"Don't sound so surprised, Elena," I say, with a forced laugh.

"Oh, I'm sorry!" she says, patting me on the shoulder. "I just always thought you were gay."

This time, from the corner of my eye, I see Jamie pick up a plate and literally hurl it at the wall. Everyone spins around in shock. Jamie stands there, surrounded by broken china. I guess there *are* more plates he can break.

"Jamie!" Mum gasps.

"There was a wasp!" he says. "We have to go."

Everyone rushes out of the house as Mum starts to clean up the crisps.

"I'll catch you up!" I call after the others.

"What are you going to do?" Mina whispers.

"I need a minute. I'll meet you at the car park by the big Currys in town."

"Yes, sir," she says, rushing away with the others.

Mum is still tidying and murmuring to herself about *kids today*. In the confusion I slip into my room. I change in record time into Jamie's clothes, grab my board from under the bed, and vault out of the window, bolting down the street.

It's fun being out dressed like this when more people are around. Nice to blend in with the crowd. I probably don't stand out as much as I think when I'm wearing the clothes Mum makes me wear, but I feel like I do. It's nice to feel normal. I wondered if I'd find it scary being in public dressed the way I like after last year, but it just feels good. I find an empty corner of the car park and try to calm down by practising backside tailslides on a low kerb (less scary than a rail), but I'm shaky and off form. Eventually I just sit down on my board.

If there's ever a time that that one book I read about anxiety should come in useful, it's now. I put my hood up, close my eyes, and try to deep-breathe to bring myself back to the moment. *It's OK*, I tell myself, *you're safe now. You're alone. You're not at an awkward birthday party hiding from your fake boyfriend. Any more. It's all OK…*

"Jay."

COME ON.

Alex is standing in front of me, nervously twisting his skateboard in his hands.

"What are you doing here?"

"I was just at the park with some friends," he says, "and I kind of hoped you'd be at the skatepark, even though you're not usually there on the weekends. But you weren't.

Obviously. So then I thought maybe you were skating somewhere else, so I went and checked out a few of the other spots around town, and then I saw you here. I'm sorry I haven't been at the skatepark. I know we should talk."

I'm not sure I can think of a worse time to admit that I'm Jamie's sister, when he's just been in my family home to celebrate my other identity's birthday, but I guess I might as well get it out of the way.

"OK," I start, "I wanted to tell you this on New Year's Eve, but then—"

"No, wait, I need to explain. That girl at the skatepark … she's not my girlfriend."

"Oh, you broke up?"

"Uh, not exactly. But, like, I don't really reply to her texts."

Great. Now I'm feeling sorry for Dani again. "That's really not the same thing, Alex. But can you just let me talk—"

"What I said on New Year's was true, even if I panicked after. I mean, I'm still panicking. Gay panicking, I guess."

"OK, we definitely need to let me talk now—"

"No! I know I shut down on you, and that was wrong. I shouldn't have ignored you and been so cold. I'm not good at talking" – he's suddenly *too* good at it, actually – "and I know it's too late and things are probably different now, but I should have just … done this."

His board clatters to the ground as he kneels down in

front of me, putting his hands on either side of my jaw and tilting my head up to kiss him. For a second his lips are on mine, before I push off the ground with my hands and roll away. This is an unexpectedly useful side effect of sitting on a skateboard.

"ALEX," I say.

He blinks, hands still in kiss position.

I've been thinking about how to say this for months, and I still don't know how to do it, so I just start talking. "I go to Heath Girls."

He looks me up and down for quite a while, as I sit with my head in my hands, terrified. Then he just says, "*Oh.*" He pauses for a moment, then sets his own skateboard next to me and awkwardly sits down.

"This is me. This is how I look. But my mum doesn't like it, so I usually wear a skirt. Jamie is my brother. You were at my birthday party earlier." Alex is staring at me like someone who's trying on glasses that are stronger than they need. I'm scared, and I keep talking in a rush: "I'm so sorry for lying to you about the homeschooling and my family. It all got out of hand, and then there was never a good time to tell you."

Alex is blinking a lot.

"This is uh … um…"

"A lot of information?"

"Yeah."

"Are you angry?"

"I don't know… You lied. I liked you, and you lied to me." He slaps a hand to his forehead. "Oh my god I should have known, you never even said *which* religion you were…"

"I'm so sorry. I lied because I was scared of anyone finding out that this is me. That's all I can say. I liked you too, and that's part of why I was so scared to tell you the truth. But I want to be your friend one day, if that's ever possible."

He nods and stands up slowly. "I think I need to…" He gestures weakly at his head.

"Think?"

"Yeah. I don't know how I…" He gestures vaguely at his chest.

"Feel?"

"Yeah. Um. OK. I'll see you. And, uh, happy birthday, I guess."

He turns away, picks up his board, and runs on to it, leaving me alone in the car park again. I put my head in my hands.

"At some point I'm going to get pretty sick of watching you two kiss."

I flinch so badly that I topple off my board and on to the concrete. Could people stop ambushing me for *five* minutes?

"*God,* Mina!"

"You and your boyfriend are pretty unobservant when you're together."

I notice the tight line her mouth is pressed into. Is she angry with me?

"He's not my boyfriend. I told him I wanted to be friends."

Mina blinks. "You did?"

"Yeah. I also told him that I'm Jennifer from Heath Girls. I told him a lot of things, actually. I think he's in shock."

"I can't believe you told him…"

"Well, I had to, didn't I?"

"I can't believe you told him you just wanted to be friends."

"I don't think I like him as much as I thought I did."

What I don't add is: *Because I like you more.*

"OK," Mina says softly, "why don't we go to mine? Get you out of here before you have any more dramatic confrontations."

"Yes, please," I say. "That's enough for one day. Is there even anyone left for me to dramatically confront?"

"Dani would probably like to slap you for kissing her boyfriend."

"Oooh, that's a good one. Do you think she's behind me?"

We turn around – and find ourselves face-to-face with my mother.

CHAPTER 23

Mum is staring at me in abject horror. She's holding a' shopping bag. She must have run out to get extra party supplies. She looks from my clothes to my hair tucked under my baseball cap to my skateboard and back again, her mouth opening and closing as she struggles for words.

For the first time ever, she's caught me doing something she doesn't like and I'm not scared. I'm angry. I can see it now: I need to stand up for myself.

Eventually she says, "What do you think you're doing?"

"Skateboarding."

"What are you wearing?"

"Clothes that I like."

"*Did you cut your hair?*"

"Actually, no. But I want to."

Tears are gathering in her eyes, and I feel my throat get tight. But this isn't about her any more. "How could you do this to me?"

"I'm not doing anything to you."

"After everything your brother and I have gone through for you…"

"What about everything I've done for *you*? I've worn those clothes you want me to wear, and I've let my hair grow even though I hate it, and it's still not enough for you."

"All of that is for *you*! So that you can fit in…"

"With who, Mum? No one cares here! Look around you! No one cares what I look like! OK, those people are kind of staring, but I think that's just because I'm yelling. Look, Mina doesn't care. The only person who cares is you!"

"You wanted this!"

"I acted like I did. But I just wanted you to like me."

Mum stares at me in shock. "This isn't … that has nothing to do with … you know this is only about keeping you safe!"

Mina steps forward. "There was a person at Heath Girls who graduated last year and looked like Jay, and they never had any trouble…"

Mum's jaw tightens. "You don't know what you're

talking about, Mina, I'm afraid. Has Jennifer told you why we moved here?"

I really thought I might get away with never having to hear or tell this story again. Mina freezes and glances at me, and it's obvious that I haven't.

"Jennifer got bullied so badly at her last school that she ended up in hospital."

Mina's hand goes to my arm.

"The bullying went on for months before that," Mum goes on. "It happened in school and online. The abuse was so bad that I had to delete all of Jennifer's social media and take away her internet access so that she wouldn't see it. The things they were saying were so horrible. It went on for a year, and her school wouldn't do anything about it. And then – last summer" – her voice cracks – "last summer, they pushed her down a flight of stairs. She broke her arm and got a concussion. All because people didn't like the way she looked. *They* cared. Do you still really think that she'll be safe if she chooses to look this way?"

In another situation, seeing Mina lost for words might be kind of funny.

Yes, that's the story of what happened. Only it's not. Not completely.

"Yeah, it was pretty bad," I say, my voice strangely calm. "I got bullied, and if I'd dressed differently maybe it wouldn't have happened. But I've been thinking. All

265

the way through school I looked like this, and nobody really seemed to mind. Sometimes somebody would say something, but it was OK, and mostly I had a good time. Then, last year, this new girl joined. She was a jerk. Her and these two other girls started saying stuff about me. But she bullied other people too; she was just a *bully*. And the stairs – yes, that sounds bad. They threw ball bearings at the top of some stairs while I was skating because they thought I'd trip. But of course I was on my board, so when I hit them I just flew... Those girls were so scared, actually. I don't think they thought through how badly I'd fall. But yes, they hated me, they hated how I looked.

"But that wasn't the worst thing, Mum. You were so upset, and you moved us away and you told me the whole reason this happened was because of how I looked, and I believed you. I've felt so guilty about it. I was so tired of you not liking anything about me and being sad that I wasn't like you. I wanted to try to make you happy. If you had just been on my side, none of that stuff would have been so bad. The truth was, you acted like I deserved it because you kind of think I did. You thought it made sense that those girls bullied me."

There's a silence and I see Mum visibly gather herself. "This isn't about what I think; this is about protecting you."

"Is it? Or do you just not like this?" I gesture at my clothes.

She can barely look at me. "I want your life to be easier, and I thought you were over your tomboy phase."

"You never asked what *I* want," I say. "You just tried to make me the way you want."

Mum has stopped crying. Her fists are clenched and her jaw is rigid. I've never seen her like this before.

"Are you … *angry?*"

"Yes," she says quietly.

Mina slips her arm into mine. "That's enough," she says. "Me and Jay are going now."

Mum looks like she's going to say something else, but she doesn't. She just gives one sharp nod and stands there as we walk away, shaking with rage.

"She's *ANGRY? At YOU?*" Mina begins, and launches into a rant. I love it.

"Mina, don't stop ranting, but I'm just going to call Jamie quickly to tell him what happened."

Mina gives me a thumbs up and keeps going: "The *audacity…*"

My hands and voice are shaking and I'm on the verge of tears, but I try to give Jamie the quickest summary possible. He tries to sound cheerful, but I can tell he's scared. I'm leaving him alone to deal with Mum. A new version of Mum, who's angry instead of sad.

That look on her face, the rage – am I ever going to be allowed back home again?

*

Ten minutes later, we wave at Mina's parents in their kitchen and hurry up the stairs as Mina continues talking in a furious whisper.

"Mina," I say, when we're in her room and she's drinking some water to recover from her rant, "what do I do?"

She thinks about it. "Well, you've got a few issues you'll have to deal with at some point."

"Yes."

"Obviously your mum. And then once Alex has cooled off, you're probably going to have to have some pretty big chats with him if you want him to forgive you."

"Yeah, I should probably get him a muffin basket or something."

"That's certainly *an* option. And then you'll have to embrace your style and deal with people double-taking at school for a few days."

"Ah."

"At some point you're going to have to give me some more detail about that traumatic stair incident and your tragic past."

"Yes, we can deep dive on that."

"But for now ... why don't we just do something nice?"

"Something nice?"

"Yeah, you've heard of nice things, right?"

"What do you want to do?"

"It's supposed to be your birthday party today. What do *you* want to do?"

I think about it. "I want to go see a movie. And then maybe get a milkshake. Then I'd like to go buy some new clothes so I don't have to borrow Jamie's all the time. But if we go walking around town and run into people, we'll have to start on all the explaining…"

"Don't worry. I have an idea."

Mina goes downstairs and talks to her parents for a while, then calls me down. Her dad is going to drive and drop us off in the next town over, where we don't know anybody.

And you know what? It's the best birthday I've ever had.

I buy a pair of jeans that aren't slightly too big for me. We go see an average movie with a lot of car chases, and Mina keeps grabbing my arm when something scary happens. We get milkshakes, and I let Mina have my Oreo one because she prefers it to her strawberry chocolate one. When her dad picks us up we're both kind of giggly and giddy. I guess it feels like … a date?

I've never been on a date. My romantic experiences so far have been limited to two brief, impassioned make-outs with a guy in a skatepark and a car park. Why is it always a park? But I think this might have been a pretty good date.

I'm onstage at a glitzy beauty pageant. I look a little out of place because I'm wearing jeans and a T-shirt instead of a bikini, but everyone is smiling kindly at me. The host, in a bright pink tuxedo, approaches me with a microphone.

"Jay, here's our question for you … describe your dream date."

269

I spot Mina in the crowd and smile.

"Today."

OK, I think it might have been the best date anyone's ever been on.

Back in Mina's room, she throws me a brightly wrapped package. I catch it against my chest and I can feel my face start to heat up as we sit next to each other on the carpet. The air feels tense in a good way. Like before a storm, but a nice non-scary storm, with tuneful thunder.

"Happy birthday, Jay."

"Aw! This almost makes up for you taking my milkshake."

"Open it."

It's two T-shirts, one from Almost and one from Zoo York – they're both skate brands, and the shirts are *so* cool.

"Mina I *love* these!"

"Oh, good! I just googled 'skateboarding shirts'. They're from the men's section, obviously, so let me know if the size isn't right. I assumed that you would be an extra small man."

"I *am* an extra small man. They're perfect. Thank you."

"Jay," says Mina, "I'm really glad I know what happened at your old school. Not so that I can feel sorry for you, but so I can understand why you were refusing to have cool hair."

I laugh and nod. I was so scared Mina would pity me – instead she just knows me better. It's nice.

Then she sits back and glances at her watch. "It's getting late. We should go to bed. Eventful day." Then, rather awkwardly, she adds, "There's a spare room across the hall where my parents have requested you sleep."

I flinch. Do her parents not trust me now I'm in boys' clothes? "Is this because I'm wearing jeans with pockets?"

"Well, it's because…" She leads me to the door of the spare room. We stand close together on either side of the threshold, and I feel that feeling – like I'm suddenly very high up, and my skin is tingling, and the air is electric. "It's because I told them I like you. And, you know, they can't let us share a room if we're dating. Rules are rules."

I can't think of anything to say, but it doesn't matter. I lean in and kiss her, and it feels like exactly the right thing to do.

CHAPTER 24

I wake up smiling in Mina's spare room. I can't believe that we kissed! I can't believe that we like each other!

Well, OK, I do see now that it's been pretty obvious for several months and I was just too nervous to accept it, but still! We kissed! It feels like everything is going to be plain sailing from here on out.

Then my phone buzzes. It's Jamie.

"Well?" I say. "How is she?"

"I don't know." He sounds worried. I feel bad that he's been left to deal with the fallout. "She won't talk to me. It really is like she's ... *angry?*" he says in disbelief.

Oh. Right. Of course nothing is going to be plain

sailing. It's going to be very spicy sailing. I have things to do:

I need to get my mother to accept my identity; I need to resolve things with Alex; and I need to pre-emptively prepare comebacks for whatever Dani is going to say when I show up at school looking like myself.

But at least I've made the decision to do it. I already feel freer.

Mina knocks and comes in smiling. I want to kiss her right away, but it really is harder to kiss people when the sun is up. She sits on the edge of the bed and her hand brushes my leg. I shift a little closer to her.

"So, what's on the agenda for today?" she asks.

"Well, I need to get dressed – in the clothes that I want."

"Great."

"I should cut my hair."

"YES."

"And, well, I guess I should talk to Mum?"

"We can deal with that."

"And I should check in on Alex." I pick up my phone and text Alex, reading it aloud to Mina as I type. "Hi, Alex, I'm so sorry again about everything. Are you OK?"

We both sit there for a few seconds after I send it, like he's going to reply straight away.

"Put the phone down; we need to give him more than twenty seconds," Mina says. "In the meantime ... haircut?"

"Are you going to do it?"

"God, no. It would look even worse than it does now. There's a barber round the corner."

"Man, I've never been to a barber with hair this long… What if they don't want to do it?"

"Well, let's invite Jamie too. They'll be less weird if there are more of us."

"I'm not sure I follow that logic."

"Strength in numbers."

An hour later, there's still no reply from Alex.

"To be fair," Mina says, "he does keep kissing you, so I'm not sure I want him to see you now that you're my … uh … you."

I feel my cheeks getting hot. What I want to say is: *"Does this mean you want to call me your girlfriend or boyfriend, or something? I think I'd be fine with either. I maybe prefer boyfriend? But what I'm saying is, if you'd like us to be going out with each other as a couple, I would also like that."*

Instead, I say, "Yeah."

Useless.

Half an hour later we meet Jamie at the nearest barber shop.

"I'm so glad we're doing this!" he yells when he sees me. "And look at your T-shirt! And these jeans! You look so good!"

"Doesn't she?" Mina says, grinning. She takes my hand and Jamie looks delighted.

"Finally."

Me and Mina just smile.

We head into the barbershop. Now, in my experience, barbers can get a little tense if they think you're a girl. But I'm ready.

"Hey," the barber says when we walk in, some bells on the door ringing. "What can I do for you?" The barber guy has a fade cut really close to the skin, a lot of tattoos, and an exciting little moustache that he's put a lot of wax in. He addresses the last bit just to Jamie.

"Actually, Jay would like a haircut," Jamie says, pushing me forward.

I start speaking very quickly: "I would like a two fading up to a four on the back and sides, with some length on the top so it's kind of undercut."

"Cool."

"And I know that – oh." With the wind taken out of my sails, I slide into the chair.

I don't want to get too sentimental about this, but watching my hair fall away is one of the best things that's happened to me this year. It's like losing a dead weight. When he finishes I feel like I'm finally looking at myself.

"Woo!" Jamie says when I stand up and turn around.

"You look *amazing*," Mina says, running her hand along

275

the shorter bristles, "and that feels great. Man, why did you ever have that mop?"

"No idea," I say, grinning, "but I never will again." And it's true. I know it. I won't ever have long hair again.

"I'm so proud," Jamie says, wiping away a fake tear. "I have the handsomest sister in the world."

I hear the door's bells ring again, and that's when I see Mina's face fall. I have my back to the entrance, and she's facing it.

"There's someone behind me, isn't there?" I whisper. She nods. I turn and see that it's Alex. But something in his eyes looks wrong. He looks frightened. "Alex? What's going on?"

"Saw you while I was walking past," he says. "Guess you haven't seen it, then."

"Seen what?"

"Check your phone."

"What are you talking about?" I say nervously. I look at my phone, but there's nothing. "Is this on socials?"

Jamie shrugs.

Mina takes out her phone and starts scrolling. Her eyes widen.

"Jay…"

"Show me."

"I don't know—"

"*Show me.*"

She turns the screen towards me. "It was posted an hour

276

ago by an anonymous account. They've tagged everybody from school."

It's two pictures of me and Alex in the car park yesterday. The first picture is us kissing. The second is just after I've pushed back from him, and you can see my face. If you've seen me at school, there's no way you wouldn't know it was me, despite the clothes. My eyes flick straight to the comments.

"Alex and JAY??"

"Why is Jay dressed like that?"

"JAY?!?"

"Looks like a guy."

The panic is rising.

I stop looking. I feel sick and my breathing is speeding up, out of my control. My head starts to spin. It's just like at my old school. How bad is it going to get?

Alex points a finger at me and snarls, "This is all your fault, Jay." He storms out of the shop, slamming the door behind him, making the barber's hands fly to his moustache in shock.

"It's not!" Mina says. "Jay, it's not— Wait!"

But I'm already running. I skate straight home as fast as I can, climb in through my window and collapse on the bed, crying. I thought I could handle this, but I can't. Everything's ruined. Everything. As I lie there sobbing, I hear the door open.

Mum walks in, looks me over, then walks out and closes the door without saying a thing.

SUMMER

CHAPTER 25

The last term of the year starts, but I'm not going in.

I hear Mum each morning when I don't come out of my room call school to tell them I'm sick. I smashed my phone the day the picture got posted online. I wanted it gone, before I started getting the same kinds of horrible texts I used to get. Jamie keeps telling me to talk to Mina, but I don't want to. I don't want to talk to anybody, not even him. Mum isn't talking to me. She lets me live in her house and eat her food, but that's it. We sit at dinner in silence while she stares at the table with that same new anger on her face, while Jamie desperately tries to get one of us to say something. I'm too tired to really care.

The first week of term slips by. I'm not even skating. I guess I'm waiting things out until the school year ends.

Mum will probably want to move soon anyway, after this. She doesn't know the details, but she knows something happened on social media. Just like she knew it would. She *was* right.

One evening I'm lying in my room with the window open, watching the sky get dark, when the door slams open.

"ENOUGH."

I yelp as Jamie barges in.

"What are you doing?"

"Stopping you from doing *this*. Get up."

"Stop yelling!"

"NO. I've tried being understanding and giving you space, but you won't even talk to me. It's time for tough love."

He tries to heave me out of bed but loses his grip and I slam into the bedside table.

"Oh, god, sorry, are you OK?"

"Yeah … ow…"

He switches back into tough love mode. "THEN GET UP. We're going outside, and we're going to see which of us can kickflip first."

"I don't want to, Jamie."

"I did not ask." He grabs my skateboard in one hand and me in the other and hauls me outside, only pausing to let me put shoes on. He pushes me into the empty road in front of our house.

"Why are we doing this, Jamie?"

He tries to do a kickflip and lands on the edge of the board, collapsing on to the concrete.

"Because ... *ow* ... it's time for you to stop lying around and running away."

"That's kind of a contradiction."

"Shut up. Do a kickflip."

I roll my eyes, but I try. I'm out of practice, though, and my heart isn't in it, so I only land with one foot on the board.

"PATHETIC!" Jamie yells, shoving me off.

I can't help it. I start to smile.

"Let me show you how it's done."

He tries again and lands on the board upside down, tumbling over forward. "Oh my god, it's so much harder than I remember."

I slide the board away from him and try again. This time it's perfect. High pop, front foot catch in the air, slam back down over the bolts and roll away clean. I feel good for a moment, even though I'm wearing baggy pyjama bottoms and an old T-shirt.

"You shouldn't have tested me," I say.

"She's back!"

"You think everything's fixed now, because I landed one kickflip?"

"No. But I think you're talking to me again, which is good."

I pop a heelflip and land that too. It *does* feel good.

"I guess."

"*I guess*," he mimics, like when we were kids.

"Don't do that."

"*Don't do that.*"

"OK, I'm not playing this game!"

"*Oooh, I'm Jay, and I'm not playing this game!*"

"You are so immature!" We say that one in unison. He knows me too well.

"What do you want me to do, Jamie?" I ask with a sigh, sitting down on my board. "Everything is ruined."

"I want you to fight back!" he says, pacing around me in circles so I have to slowly rotate to keep eyes on him. "I want to go back to last week, when you cut your hair and stood up to Mum and came clean to Alex and bought the clothes you wanted to wear and finally got together with Mina."

"Yeah, well, none of that worked out so well, did it?"

"Are you kidding? Sure, it was a pretty dramatic end to a haircut. But other than that, I think it was all pretty awesome."

"You're ridiculous. Everyone's talking about me online again; I'm back to being the weird kid who looks like a boy."

"Or are you the person who made out with the coolest guy in school and doesn't care what anybody thinks?"

"I doubt he's the coolest guy in school any more, though, is he?"

"Yeah, he is. If anything, he's cooler."

"What?"

Jamie is practically bouncing with excitement. I recognize that look – he has gossip to reveal. In spite of myself, I feel a little excited too.

"Let me tell you what happened today. Jay, it was so cool. In our form group, someone made a joke about Alex kissing a girl who looks like a boy." I wince, but Jamie holds a hand up to show he's not finished. "And Alex just goes, 'Yeah, well, I'm gay; it's kind of what I'm into', and everyone was like, 'Whaaaat?', and the guy who made the joke, Dom, goes, 'Are you kidding?', and he says, 'No', and the guy said, 'Well, don't come on to me', and Alex said, 'I'm gay, not desperate', which was uncharacteristically sharp from Alex and I think actually cut Dom pretty deep because everybody laughed. By lunch everyone at both schools knew, and everyone thinks Alex is even deeper and more interesting now they know that he's gay. Which is ridiculous; he's still basic."

"He came out? He told everybody?"

"Yeah, he did. And, Jay, everyone's cool with it."

"I can't believe he did it. I mean, everyone knows I go to Heath Girls, so he didn't even have to tell anyone that he's gay."

"Jay, look at you. Anybody that kisses you is gay."

That really cracks me up. "Yeah, actually, that's kind of what I think too."

"He said he was gay, and that was that. Of course, Dani's friends are still up in arms on her behalf. He did cheat on her." I think that one over.

"I know Mum's been telling you that you need to fit in to be safe, but that's just because she doesn't really know what our world is like. At our last school, I think you got really, really unlucky and you met some people who were horrible. I'm not saying that there's never going to be anybody else like that in your life. But they're wrong, and you're right, and you're going to be surrounded by people you do fit with. People like me and Mina. You shouldn't have to hide."

"That was a really rousing speech."

"Thank you, I've been working on it."

"So … what are people saying about me?"

"Well, Dani hates you. But that's not new."

"Yeah, but now I guess she hates me separately from how I dress. Which is kind of nice."

"Exactly. Dani hates you for who you are as a person," he says, with a comforting shoulder pat. "And everyone else was just surprised, I think. Like, yes, people might stare at you for a while. But it's going to be obvious to everybody that this is just *you*. You look the way you're meant to."

"And … what about Mina?"

He hesitates. "She's really angry. Ghosting her because you panicked was not the most mature thing to do."

"Yeah, no, I know…"

"Pretty wild, actually. When you'd finally got together. Or started holding hands, at the very least."

"Yes, thank you, I get it."

"But I think she'll forgive you if you just talk to her."

I shake my head. As if anything could be that simple. "Do you really believe that?" I snap. "That I can walk into school and people will stare a bit and then forget about it, and Mina will forgive me?"

"Yes. I believe that the world hasn't ended as much as you think it has. If you think that everything is ruined for ever, and everybody hates you and thinks you're weird, then you're thinking like Mum."

That makes me think.

He's right. I hate that he's always right. Doesn't *he* ever get sick of it?

"OK. So what do you think I should do?"

"Well, the Summer Dance is coming up. If this was a high school movie, you'd show up in an awesome suit and everybody would be like, 'Oh my god, look at Jay!' and then you and Mina would dance together."

"But this isn't a high school movie."

Jamie raises his eyebrows and grins.

"Jamie. No. Come on. Be serious."

CHAPTER 26

"Hello!" Jamie beams at the slightly bemused shop assistant. "I would like to purchase this same suit, one size down, for my beloved sibling."

He puts a hand on my shoulder and pushes me slightly forward like he's offering me to the sales guy and waves at the suit he insisted on wearing. He said it was the only way to show the people in the store what we wanted. I think he just likes wearing a suit.

"Matching suits? That's really cute," Sales Guy says, taking us over to the rack of suits.

"Yeah, we're adorable," I say.

He hands me a jacket to try on.

"There you go, the shoulders are perfect," Sales Guy says, holding his palms on either side of me. "See how they line up with your body exactly? This shirt's the same size as the jacket. And these trousers look right," he says, holding a pair up against me.

"Thank you!"

"Go try everything on, man. You don't see a lot of brothers that get on as well as you two."

Jamie grins at me. "Let's go, bro."

Sales Guy was one hundred per cent convinced that I'm a boy, but Changing Room Girl is less sure.

"Uh, the women's changing rooms are on floor two," she says.

"But these are gender-neutral changing rooms," I say, pointing at the sign, which doesn't say men or women on it.

"But it's the men's floor."

"But they're gender neutral," Jamie echoes.

She sighs. "Fine," she says, letting us past.

"God, people are so weird," Jamie says, shaking his head pityingly.

"They really are, aren't they?" I say, as he sits on the waiting bench and I head into a cubicle.

"They're all individual cubicles, anyway. It's not like you have to get changed in one huge room where you all watch each other and then wrestle, or something."

"Even if you did have to wrestle you'd probably want to split that up by weight class, not gender," he says

289

thoughtfully. "I think Tom Proctor could break me in half, gender aside."

"Can everybody stop talking about how strong and muscular and beautiful Tom Proctor is? Mina better not have fallen in love with him while I've been useless. I'll have to wrestle him if she has."

"Try on your suit."

I close the door and get changed, then turn around to look in the mirror.

I look *good*. I'm not saying that in an arrogant way, it's just true. The suit fits perfectly, not like the oversized ones you see most teenage boys in. The light blue suits me. The shoulders hug mine perfectly, and the trousers stop right at the top of my shoes, like it was made for me. Smiling, I open the door.

"Jay, you look so *good*!" Jamie whoops. "I mean, this is incredible, you look almost as good as me!"

He grabs me so that we're both in the mirror together. I actually think I look slightly better, but I'll let him have this.

"We look like we're in a boy band."

"Mina is going to absolutely swoon!"

"Are you sure we shouldn't text her to let her know that I'll be at the dance?"

"Don't be ridiculous. You'd lose the element of surprise."

"Is the element of surprise really something you want when you're trying to get someone to forgive you?"

"Why wouldn't it be? If you really surprise them, they won't remember what you did wrong."

"Well, I guess I have to trust you since you're the one with the girlfriend." Jamie and Elena are going out "officially" now. He seems besotted. He's always telling me about funny things she's said, and how much they make each other laugh. Before, I don't know what I would have said if someone had asked me who the perfect girl for Jamie would be, but now I realize it's Elena.

"Well, you'd better go take that off so we can buy it. I don't think they like scanning the tags while you're still wearing it."

"Good point."

I slip back into the changing room and close the door. "Hey, listen," I say, suddenly feeling totally shy, "thank you."

"Don't worry about it. Matching suits makes us *both* look cooler."

"No, I mean, thank you for everything this year. For saving my skateboard, and giving me your old clothes, and looking out for me, even when I was lying to you and being kind of a jerk."

"Aw. Well. I'm your big brother; I do those things."

"I just feel like this year's been all about me, you know? I don't know how to pay you back."

"We can take it in turns being the main character. One day I'll probably need you. When that day comes, be ready."

"You're making it sound like you're going to take my firstborn child, or something."

"Maybe I am. Maybe I am."

Mum is sitting in the living room when we walk in, and I'm ready for her to just keep acting like I'm a ghost. But suddenly she speaks.

"You went shopping."

Me and Jamie both look around for who she's speaking to, before we realize that it has to be us. Or actually, me. She's looking at me.

"Yeah, we did."

"What did you get?"

"Um … I got a suit. For the dance."

"It matches mine," Jamie says.

Mum nods slowly. I feel like I'm about to be put on trial.

The courtroom is full of whispering people, who fall silent when Mum slams down her tiny little hammer. (What are those called? I'm sure they don't call them tiny little hammers. Or maybe they do. It's what they are.)

"I find the defendant guilty of purchasing gender inappropriate formal wear. I sentence you to wear a dress for ever."

"Can I appeal?"

"For questioning me, I sentence you to wear heels as well."

"But—"

"That's added lipstick on. You want to keep challenging me? You want me to throw in some tasteful pearl earrings?"

292

Jamie and me are both poised for some kind of explosion, but it doesn't come.

"I wish I understood," she says with a sigh. "I wish you both felt like you could tell me things."

Well, *this* is unexpected. There's a pause as Jamie and I look cautiously at each other.

"It's OK," I say awkwardly.

"I wanted you two to have safe, easy lives. I tried so hard to make that happen." She laughs shakily. "I always thought I knew what my children would be like, for some reason. I always thought my daughter would be like me. But that isn't you, is it?"

"No."

She nods again.

"Are you angry at me?"

She looks surprised. "No."

"That day in the car park, and since then, you've seemed so angry. I thought you hated me."

"I *was* angry," she says quietly, "but at myself because you were right. I didn't understand why you wanted to be so different from me, and from how people are supposed to be – or so I thought. And I didn't try to understand. I'll try harder. And … I'm sorry. Sorry that I made you feel what happened before was your fault. It wasn't."

It's the first time I've ever heard her say sorry.

"Thanks, Mum."

She pats me on the shoulder. It's kind of awkward, but as she does it, she says:

"Jay."

CHAPTER 27

"OK," Jamie says, straightening my jacket for the hundredth time, "are you ready?"

"Not at all. Are you sure we should do this? There's someone at this dance who *really* hates me, a bunch who mid-level hate me, a few people who *might* hate me, and everyone is guaranteed to stare at me."

"What could go wrong?"

"Do you actually want me to answer that?"

"No, we'd be here all night. Let's go."

I take a deep breath and follow him to the front door.

"Wait."

Mum is standing in the hallway, holding some pink

flowers. She steps forward and threads a flower into Jamie's buttonhole, then one into mine. I think it might be the first time she's ever treated us both the same.

"And the other two you can give to your ... dates."

Jamie holds his excitedly. I slip mine into my pocket, already picturing Mina tearing it up in front of me in a fit of righteous anger.

"Thank you, Mum," I say.

"Yep." She nods and smiles. It's still awkward as hell, but it's kind of nice. "I almost forgot: let me take a photo of you both!"

She takes us outside. I try to ignore the other kids I kind of know from school who are walking by, even though I'm sure I hear someone say "Is that Jay?" The first few pictures are incredibly awkward, but they get slowly more ridiculous as we go. Even Mum is laughing when I manage to hold Jamie up in the air for the last one.

"OK," she says, "have fun tonight. Be safe. Don't forget to text... Oh, never mind. You're ten minutes down the road. Have a great time."

And she walks back into the house.

"Wow," Jamie says as we start off down the street, "she really is changing."

She really is. At dinner the other day she mentioned she's started doing counselling through work for anxiety. I'd never thought about parents doing that kind of thing, and I'm really proud of her.

Jamie is completely overexcited the whole way there. "Oh, man, tonight is gonna be so cool. I'm gonna give Elena this flower, and she's going to look so pretty, and we're gonna dance, and everyone's going to be so well dressed, which you know I always appreciate, and then you're going to give that flower to Mina, and *you'll* both dance..."

"Or Dani's gonna slap me in the face, Alex is gonna yell at me, and Mina is going to set my little flower on fire."

"I thought we weren't listing what could go wrong, but I'm pretty sure a teacher would step in and prevent at least some of that. Either way, you're facing everything head on. Taking the bull by the horns. No more hiding."

"No more hiding," I repeat, even though I feel like maybe hiding would be a good idea.

"Jamie!" Elena is waiting for him outside the gates. She looks really nice in her dress.

Jamie immediately drops to one knee and dramatically offers her the little pink flower. She delightedly puts it in her hair.

"This is so sweet," she says. "We look like we're all one big date, with our matching flowers. No, that would be wrong – you're related. But you look really handsome, Jay. Or pretty. Would you like to be pretty? You look nice. Jamie, you look nicer. Sorry, Jay, no offence."

"That's OK, Elena, thank you."

I can definitely hear people saying "Is that Jay?" as we walk into the gym together, but after the first few times I stop minding. It's like Jamie said: people are just surprised, and if they're anything other than that, it's their problem. I like how I look tonight. I just look straight ahead, trying not to look too hard for Mina. Or Alex. Or Dani.

The dance is in the gym. I knew what the decorations were going to be from all the Planning Committee meetings I attended, but I didn't think the transformation would look this good. Dani may technically be my worst enemy, but she does have an eye for colour. The pink and blue accessories pop out against the background, and with everyone dressed in the same colours the coordination is really pleasing to look at. Looking around, I also notice that not everybody stuck to the pink for girls and blue for boys rule: there are girls in blue dresses, and a few boys in pink suits, which makes me feel a bit more relaxed about breaking the rules. There's an older kid from the boys' school with long hair and a purple suit, and we smile at each other for a second. I notice a few other people in purple too. I was kind of worried Dani might have hired security to make sure nobody messed around. People are definitely still looking at me, but as the music gets louder and people group up with their friends, they pay me less and less attention — and to be honest, it seems like they're too busy scoping out each other's outfits and hoping people are looking at *them*. Me, Jamie and Elena chat and I keep an eye out for Mina, Alex, and Dani.

Of course, *everybody* looks when Ms George shrieks: "JAY! YOU LOOK AMAZING!" She sprints across the gym and grabs me in a hug.

"Thanks, Ms George!"

"That's OK; I'm sorry for yelling." She's wearing a pink dress with a cool blue shawl-sort-of-thing over the top.

"You look great too."

"Thanks! I love these dances," she says, and then switches suddenly into teacher mode: "We missed you last week. You'd better be back in class on Monday."

"I will, I promise."

"OK, good. Let's start having our weekly meetings again. Lunchtime, if you want, since you're not meeting Hugo. In fact, you probably haven't heard, but he's decided to stop teaching at the end of the year and retrain as a personal trainer." Ms George clearly thinks this is a good choice. "You kids have fun. Elena, I'm going to go ask your brother to play something less good; he's using the hits too soon."

She bounces off.

"It's strange that you're friends with a teacher," Elena says, slinging a friendly arm around my shoulders.

"I know."

"Hey, Jay," Jamie says, "look."

It's Mina. She's just walked in with a few other girls

from our year, and she looks incredible. She's wearing the dress she bought that day Mum took us shopping, but I can see she's made some slight alterations to it, giving the skirt more interesting angles. It's so perfectly her, it takes my breath away even more than the first time. I can't believe I haven't seen her in so long. I can't believe I've been so scared and pushed her away. She's staring at me in what looks like shock, mouth slightly open. I square my shoulders and start to walk towards her … then a crowd of people push past, and she's suddenly gone.

I turn around to Jamie and Elena, confused. "How did she do that?"

Elena nods wisely. "She probably shimmered off to the girls' bathroom. That's where we go when there's trouble."

"Shimmered?"

"I'll go look for her." Elena disappears into the crowd.

"*So close,*" I say to Jamie. "I really thought that was going to be my 'beg for forgiveness' moment."

"I guess we'll have to wait," Jamie says. "Elena will find her. Come hang out with the Toms."

Tom Proctor, to my surprise, is wearing a pink suit. The colour has never looked so masculine; he looks like he's about to burst out of the thing like the Hulk. I really hope puberty is done with this guy, he can't take any more.

"Jay, you look sick," he says, slapping me a meaty high five.

"Thanks, Tom," I say. "Great suit."

"Thank you! I'm not sure about how the sleeves fit; I think they make my arms look small."

"I think that would be hard."

"Jay! I love your suit," says Little Tom, round glasses glinting. God, that kid's cute. He actually looks older than when I last saw him, but he still has the same shy, silly energy.

"Thanks, Tom! You look great too." He's wearing a navy suit that makes him look sharp, but also like he might be some sort of junior accountant. It works.

"Jay! I think Mina went that way!" Jamie points across the room, towards the stage where the DJ is playing. I see a flash of a dress that could be Mina's and set off in pursuit. On the way, a few people from class tell me I look good, which is really nice but makes me lose track of her. Now I'm stranded in a group of people I don't know.

Oh no. I *do* know one of them.

We're too close together for me not to say anything.

"Hi, Dani."

She looks incredible, obviously. She's wearing a simple, floor-length, figure-hugging, dusky pink dress that cinches at the waist, and she has one of those little bags in one hand, gripped by recently manicured nails. I can feel her circle of girlfriends whispering to each other as they form a loose circle around us. Millicent. Bertha. Prudence. WHY did I never learn any of their names? I'm trapped.

"I like your French tips," I say, gesturing at Dani's hands.

I think that actually buys me a few seconds, because she seems too surprised that I know what a French tip is to immediately insult me. "Listen, Dani," I continue while she's stunned, "I'm just gonna be upfront and say that I'm really sorry for kissing your boyfriend."

She regains her composure. She looks me up and down disparagingly. One eyebrow cocks like a pistol. The insult is coming. I jump in.

"Dani, before you say anything, I've also been wanting to say: you are *really* good at insults. I don't know if anyone's ever actually told you that before, but you seriously have a gift. You could do stand-up or write coffee table books if you wanted to. You really have a talent. Though you're currently using it for unchecked cruelty."

There's a collective "Oooohhhhh" from the people around us. Dani stares.

"But, um, that doesn't take away from the fact that I really am sorry. And maybe now I've hyped up your insult skills too much for you to say it – this is probably a lot of pressure – but please go ahead. Fire away."

Dani licks her lips. I've never seen her with stage fright before. I keep talking like a freight train.

"It's OK," I continue rambling. "Don't worry, I know you've still got it. You can come find me later if you want. But seriously, I am sorry for the whole thing with Alex. And I'm sorry that the picture got sent around."

Me and Dani both glance at her cronies when I say

that, and they all look at each other nervously. I'd guessed it would be one of them, and it looks like Dani has too.

"And I'll stay away from you for ever. Again, great nails. OK, I'll go now."

I worm my way out of the circle. Dani catches my wrist with one sharp hand, and I turn slowly back.

"You look like a ring bearer."

I can't help it. It's funny! I start laughing. "That was good."

She starts laughing too. Just for a second before she can stop herself. "Go away."

"Yes, ma'am."

I breathe out for the first time in at least five minutes as I snake through the crowd away from her group. I look around hopelessly. I can't see Mina, or Jamie and Elena, or the Toms. I step outside into the grass area just outside the gym. Points to Dani and her team: they've made it look delightful and magical through the liberal use of fairy lights.

It's nice out here. Quiet.

And I'm finally alone.

"Jay."

Or *not* so alone. I know the voice and take a deep breath before I turn around: "Hey, Alex."

He's perched in the lowest branch of a tree, surrounded by fairy lights. He looks great in a midnight-blue suit, with the tie rakishly tugged loose and the shirt already untucked.

He's wearing skate shoes, which I think looks really cool, but Jamie would say "breaks the rules of suiting". (But he says a lot of things.) Alex doesn't look angry at me exactly, but my adrenaline rises remembering how he yelled at me last time we saw each other. I've practised what to say a hundred times, but what comes out is:

"How's things?"

"They're good. Now."

"I'm really sorry everything happened the way it did. And for lying to you."

He nods. "I was really pissed, but I guess I kind of … get it. I used Dani to hide who I was too. I was so scared of people knowing about me. I've known I'm gay for a really long time … and you were the first person it felt real with."

"I hope that wasn't too confusing," I say slowly, "with me not being … you know."

"At first, kind of. But, like, I'm gay. I liked this," he says, waving at me. "It doesn't actually feel that complicated. Not that I still like you, to be clear."

"Oh, no, I didn't assume…"

"Yeah, that ship has kind of sailed, you know?"

"Yeah, for sure, thank you."

"Yeah." He stares moodily into the distance for a while.

"I think it's really cool that you came out to everybody," I say. "It made me feel like I could show up dressed like this. So … *thanks*."

He actually blushes, grinning. "I even told my dad, you know."

"You told your dad! How did he react?"

"Absolute surprise. But I think he'll come around."

"Man, we've got to talk about your dad and my mum some time. Compare notes."

"I was going to go hit some rails in town next weekend."

"Cool."

"I'm saying, come with me, if you want. Hang out."

"Oh! Right. Really?"

"Yeah, you know," he says, kicking the ground, "it's nice having a friend who skates. So … friends?"

"Friends," I say, grinning. "Are you coming back in?"

"Nah, maybe later. See ya."

He leans back against the tree trunk to look beautiful and cool and a bit sad. I want to insist he come in and hang out with us, but the friendship is very new and I don't want to push it.

I reluctantly walk back inside and bump straight into Little Tom.

"Oh! Hey, Tom."

"Hi!!!" His eyes are wide and he looks flushed. He can't quite meet my eye.

"Why are you so nervous?"

"Nothing!"

Then I notice that he's staring straight past me and has his eyes fixed on Alex. Oh. OH.

"Sorry," he says, still looking at Alex, "did you say something?"

"Little Tom, you should go talk to him."

"What?"

"You're looking at Alex, right? Not just admiring the fairy lights?"

"Oh … um … yes."

"It might not be immediately clear because of his aloof vibe, but I think he'd really like it if you went and talked to him."

"Are you sure? He always looks so…"

"Intimidating, yeah, it's the cheekbones. But really he's just some guy in a tree." I pick up two cups of juice from the drinks table and hand them to Little Tom. "Go take him a drink and ask him a ton of questions. He'll like that, I promise."

He takes the juice and puffs out his chest.

"Thanks, Jay."

"You're welcome."

I spot Jamie and make my way over.

"Is Little Tom into Alex?" I ask.

"I had never considered the possibility before, but now that you say it, *yes*, it's completely obvious."

"How about that."

"How *about* that."

The music changes suddenly to a slow song and people start to couple up. Elena is waving Jamie over, but he hangs back.

"Have you seen her yet?"

"No. Still no," I say, sighing, "but you go, dance with Elena. I'll hang out here." I gesture at … the wall.

Jamie pats me on the shoulder and shimmies over to Elena.

I lean against my cool single-people wall and watch everyone else dance and sway to the music. To anyone who sees me, it probably looks a little sad, but it's kind of nice. I don't feel *lonely*, just sort of removed from the situation. Jamie and Elena look incredibly cute with their matching flowers. Dani and Tom Proctor are dancing together, looking like a couple who have been genetically engineered in a lab. As more and more people move on to the dance floor and the space around it clears, I see her.

Mina.

She's leaning against the wall too, looking at everybody else. Then it's like she feels my eyes on her, and she looks up.

I quickly walk over, just in case she's thinking about running away again.

"Hi."

"Hello."

"I wanted to text you. But I kind of broke my phone. And then I was scared."

"Scared that I'd be angry at you for totally ditching me and disappearing for a week?"

"Yes."

307

"Yeah, I was and I am."

"I'm sorry."

She nods. I feel like it's not enough.

"I brought you a flower," I say, reaching into my pocket and pulling out a crushed pink flower.

"Wow. What happened to it?"

"Um, well, I couldn't find you, so it's sort of been riding around in my pocket for a while."

"I think giving someone a flower this mangled is more of a threat than a compliment."

"Here," I say, taking the flower out of my buttonhole and swapping it for the crushed one, "you can have the nice one. I'll take … whatever this is."

"I didn't say I wanted your little flower."

"Do you really not? Who doesn't want a little flower?"

She thinks about it, and then reluctantly threads it into the bracelet she's wearing. "You need to do the big speech," she says.

"The big speech?"

"Yeah, where you tell me how you feel about me and apologize for hurting me and promise not to do it again."

"OK. Right. Um. Here?"

"Where else?"

"No, you're right, here is fine. Should we slow dance? While I do it?"

"We'll dance after. *If* it's good."

"OK."

I take a deep breath.

"Mina, I shouldn't have shut you out. Since I met you, you've made me feel amazing. You get me. I've never had that before. I just panicked when I thought everything was going wrong and I couldn't handle it. I ran away from you. And I won't do that again. From the first time we met, I haven't been able to keep my eyes off you. I always want to talk to you, and I always want to keep finding out more about you, and whenever we say goodbye, I can't wait to see you again. It took me a while to work out that all this means that I like you ... I like you so much. I want to go out with you. If ... I may."

She cracks up. "If you *may?*"

"Can we be serious, for one minute?"

"Who says 'if I may'?"

"Grammatically correct people."

She keeps giggling. I shift uneasily.

"So was it good? The speech? Do we dance?"

"We dance."

Thank god it's a long song. We join the other couples, and I slip my arms around her waist while she wraps hers around my shoulders. Jamie gives me a thumbs up, and I grin back.

"You may, by the way," she says, smiling at me.

"I may?"

"We may. Go out."

"Well, *that's* a relief. I really wasn't sure what you were going to say. Before the dancing, to be fair. Then I kind of figured it was in the bag."

"I've been hitting on you for months. You really took a while to catch on, and I was not subtle."

"I didn't want to make assumptions, in case you were hitting on me as a friend."

"Right," she says, grinning and shaking her head. "Well, at least we're finally here. You're my girlfriend. Or … boyfriend?"

"Kinda both, kinda neither?"

"Partner?"

"Don't say that, it makes me think of cowboys."

"Hot."

"I … don't have a word for it, I guess. For me. Is that OK?"

"That's very OK. You'll find one if you need it. Can we stop talking now?"

"We can stop talking now," I say, and lean in for the kiss.

It's hard to describe a really great kiss, isn't it?

All I can really say: it's perfect.

We're perfect.

ACKNOWLEDGEMENTS

Thank you to my friends who read this while I was editing it and said encouraging things that stopped me from hurling my laptop into the sea. Amy, Dad, Jodie, Kat, Max, Mum, Rachel, Sarah K, Sarah R.

Thank you to my incredible agent Alice Williams for seeing what I was trying to do before I'd managed to do it, and then helping me do it. Thank you also to the fantastic teams of editors at Scholastic Books for seeing what I was trying to do and then helping me do it with apostrophes in the right places. Thanks to the whole team behind pitching, editing and distributing this book for taking a chance on it and on me!

Thank you to Penguin WriteNow for giving me the confidence to write more than 2000 words of this.

Thank you to Fender. You do not care what I do for a living, but you are a good dog.

Thank you to everybody!

And thank YOU for reading this!

Ruby Clyde is a writer and comedian based in South London. Ruby grew up in Brixton and Tulse Hill, and has now moved one hill over, to Herne Hill. They perform with critically acclaimed musical comedy double act Shelf for both adults and children. This is Ruby's first book, which is exciting (for them). As well as writing, Ruby enjoys playing the guitar, weightlifting, music, videogames and hanging out with Fender the dog. As a teenager they loved skateboarding, but they can't really kickflip any more.